I0787670

They're All Named Poppy

Sarah L. Pratt

They're All Named Poppy

Radical Bookshop and Press
4838 Richard Road SW, Suite 300
Calgary, AB T3E 6L1
Canada

FIC029000 - Fiction, Short Stories

Editor: Charlotte Hayes-Clemens
Cover Design: Lexie Angelo

Typeset in Bookmania

ISBN-13: 978-1-990201-21-9

Printed in the United States

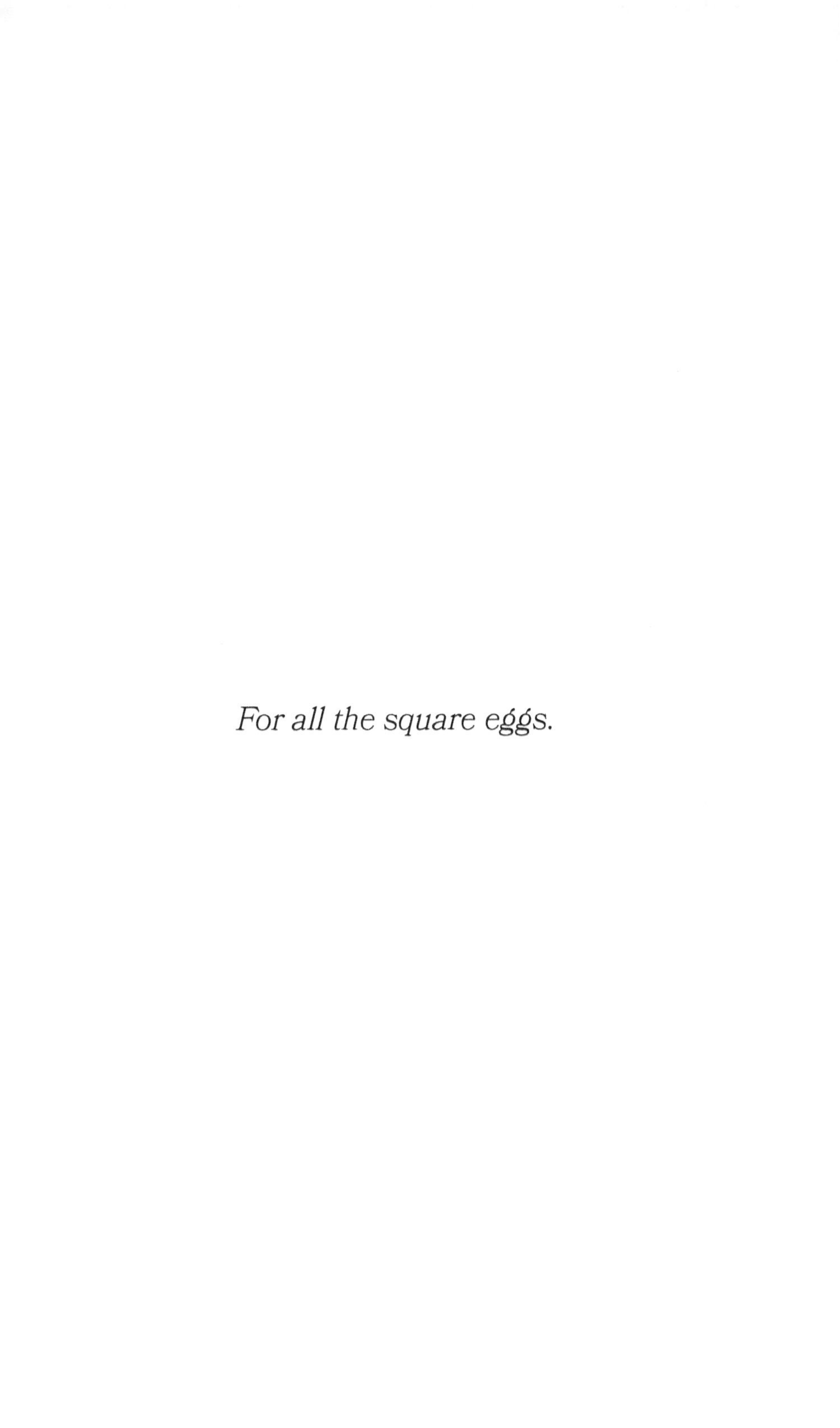

For all the square eggs.

THEY'RE ALL NAMED POPPY

Dana drops the inhaler into a white paper bag, folds the top, attaches the prescription receipt, and seals the package with her green stapler—a sleek Swingline reached for so often, her hand locates it intuitively, like a detachable appendage. "That'll be $15.80."

"Can I get sugar-testing strips with that?" Ben asks.

Orders them casually, like fries. He's not diabetic. Dana isn't even sure he has asthma. "People don't use the strips much anymore. Swing by tomorrow afternoon? I can have some by then."

"Oh..." He rubs his hands together in his peculiar way, fingers and thumbs splayed back so only his palms touch. "Thing is, I'm worried about my blood glucose. Feels high."

"I'll have the strips tomorrow."

"Right, okay... Just throw in some selenium for today." He snatches the bottle off the shelf without looking. Muscle memory, just like her stapler. He knows the precise location of each vitamin, mineral, and snake oil tincture on the shelf.

"You know you're going to pee this out, right?" Her phone hums in her pocket, and again a second later. HOok notifications. Tacky to have them buzzing in her lab coat, but it's never too early to start planning one's evening. "I doubt you have a selenium deficiency."

"My thyroid is enlarged." He tips his scruffy chin back, exposing a pale throat.

"I'm not a doctor."

"Sure you are," he says, voice struggling through his compressed larynx. "Your degree is on the wall."

"PharmD, not MD." She pulls her phone out, knowing this could backfire hard. "I'm beta testing an app a physiotherapist friend of mine helped develop." She dismisses the message from last night's hit and run—*Ino I'm not supposed 2 do this but u wanna hang out again?*—and holds her camera up to Ben. "I take your picture, and SKINR shows the anatomy underneath. See?"

Ben takes her phone and traces out his digitally mapped interior. "Wicked."

"It isn't a diagnostic tool," she warns.

"Looks enlarged."

"You do not have a goitre."

He smiles wide enough to reveal a crooked canine, but his eyes remain fixed on her screen. "Can you share this with me?"

Dana takes back her phone and is about to send the link to Ben's email when she pauses, glaring down at him. "If you walk in here tomorrow with some new fatal affliction, I swear..."

"I won't. Got enough real things killing me."

Ben swallows and Dana observes the smooth roll of his Adam's apple between the tendons and cartilage that comprise the complex structures of the throat and neck. A good neck. The neck of any twenty-six-year-old man. If only he weren't so clammy and nervous.

He slides a fifty across the counter and Dana hands him his change. Always cash. No insurance. He tucks the bag into the pocket of his shabby pea coat.

"Be gone," she says.

"See you tomorrow, Dana."

Ben waves to her cashier, Marge, as he passes through the swinging door into the late afternoon sun. He's got a funny way of walking, head turtled into the collar of his coat. The frayed hems of his jeans straggle behind his sneakers and she imagines them leaving thready tracks in the lingering snow from last week's flurry. She's fond of Ben. But Dana likes a man she can look up to, and at five and a half feet she'd be staring right into his eyes, which he would hate.

That, and he's practically a child.

Height and youth aside, Ben is a loyal customer. In addition to weekly complaints of everything from anthrax to Dutch elm disease, he fancies himself gluten, casein, and latex intolerant—and Dana is one of the few pharmacists in town that does compounding. This old-fashioned practice of providing custom medications happens to be the part of her job she likes best. In her romantic moments she fancies herself an apothecary, working with raw materials: powders, gels, solvents, dyes, stabilizing agents, and vegan gelatin capsules. Bespoke potions and salves to ease the ills of the millennial generation and their progeny.

Most of the time she isn't that romantic, and Ben is a pain in the ass.

Over the last four years, they've established relationship parameters. Topics of discussion are limited to bodily functions and pharmacology. She, on the raised platform of the dispensary. Him, on the other side. In their entire acquaintance, they have never stood on equal footing.

"Pick up for Partridge?"

"Hmm?" Dana snaps out of her musings to find a sturdy woman looking her in the eye, even from low ground. "Yes, of course."

Dana retreats to the locked narcotics cabinet. She remembers this customer and pauses with the plastic bottle of carefully documented Oxy-Neo in her hand. Theodora Partridge doesn't live in this quadrant of Calgary, has never filled a prescription at Dana's pharmacy before, and her first is for narcotics. Not a red flag. Not exactly. Dana received the script through Alberta's regulated tracking program. She even phoned the prescribing doctor's office to verify. By the book, but something about this doesn't pass the sniff test.

"I'll just need to see a piece of..." Dana trails off as she approaches the counter, seeing that Ms. Partridge has her driver's licence out and ready. "You've done this before?"

Partridge stiffens in her Patagonia vest. "I know the routine."

"You've taken Oxy-Neo previously?" Dana says, injecting a bolus of careful neutrality into her tone.

"Herniated discs."

"This is a new prescription. And the first I've filled for you."

Partridge slaps her licence on the counter. "Everyone knows you need to show ID for narcotics."

"Have you discussed alternatives with your physician? Back pain in particular responds well to transcutaneous electrical—"

"You want to talk to my doctor, review my treatment plan?" Partridge retorts. "I'm waiting for an MRI, okay? Then I'll probably wait for surgery. If a TENS machine was the answer, you think I'd be taking this poison?"

"It's important that you're aware of the options." Dana firmly slides Partridge's ID back across the counter. "This medication is habit forming."

"I'm not a junkie."

It's time to back off, to surrender. Which isn't to say Dana's instincts are wrong. Addicts rarely present as junkies. They have good insurance, dress smart, and speak well. They are desperate, and they are convincing.

Ms. Partridge squints. "Is there an actual problem here?"

Dana's jaw tightens. The future of her career could hinge on this moment. Partridge doesn't realize or doesn't care. In the current climate of opiate panic, having your paperwork in order won't prevent your licence from being suspended in the event of an overdose. If the college of pharmacists decides action must be taken, that's it; game over. And the business is all Dana has. Dotted I's and crossed T's can't mask the unmistakable whiff of desperation wafting off Ms. Partridge.

"I'm here to help," Dana says, ringing the prescription through.

"Mission accomplished." Partridge snatches the bag, mouth pressed shut in irritation, and...something else. Amusement? Derision? At the uptight pharmacist following the rules?

In the end, Dana had no grounds on which to refuse service.

Still, the interaction sticks in her craw, and the remainder of the day passes in the slow, steady turn of a mill, grinding every second into fine powder.

A buzz in her pocket at 8 p.m. She reads the message.

U ghosting me?

Revulsion scoops her up and slams her down. That chiselled freak is violating the spirit, if not the letter, of HOok's community standards. She can block him manually. She could have done it the second she left his apartment, his sweat still cooling on her skin. Blocking him didn't seem as urgent as racing home for a shower, his shiny eyes and Euclidean muscles already fading in her memory, replaced by flashbacks of abundant armpit hair, hammertoes, and his habit of prefacing every spoken thought with *Okay, so...* But in spite of those understandable turn-offs, it's definitely her, not him.

"Dana?" Marge jars her out of a neurotic spiral. "Closing time. You're here awful late."

Dana drops a dozen boxes of expired glycerin suppositories in the trash and notes the waste in her inventory app. She doesn't tell Marge that she often comes in after closing and works quietly into the night. Often enough that she knows every shadow like a lifelong friend. She can hum along to the ticking backbeat of the heating system, detect the faint smell of curing concrete when it rains, and her feet recognize the texture and wear of every floor tile. It's the most intimate relationship Dana has.

"Catching up on odds and ends," she says. "I'll hit the lights back here. You need a lift home?"

"No need to go crosstown for me, chickie. I'll take the people's chariot."

"Actually, I'm headed that direction."

"At this hour?" Marge keys in the alarm code and locks the door. "Hot date?"

"Tepid errand," Dana says as they stroll across the parking lot. "Not into the dating scene right now."

"Pretty young gal oughta be playing the field. It's easy. Even my sister is on Tinder."

"Forty is not that young."

"Neither is Gwen," Marge grunts, dropping into the passenger seat of Dana's Ford Focus. "Seventy-year-old widow with twenty-five-year-old boys sending her pictures of their genitals. Their genitals. Feature that?"

Dana starts the car and pulls into the sleepy Bridgeland traffic.

"I googled it," Marge says, fussing with her shoulder belt. "A fetish thing. Young fellas figure the way to juice up Granny's panties is a picture of their—"

"Genitals. I get it, Marge." Dana turns left at a four-way stop. "But it's not just the young ones. When I was on Tinder, plenty of old guys sent me dick pics."

"Well, heck." Marge squeezes Dana's wrist. "I'm sorry, chickie. I don't envy you."

Dana is not sorry.

On an idly curious Sunday afternoon, she hooked up with one of those elderly penii, and while the staff was not exactly mighty, he was an undeniable wizard in bed. That octogenarian went down on her like he just about invented it. If she could ever be with the same man more than once, it would be Gandalf the Grey.

"Oh!" Marge claps her hands as they pull up in front of her duplex. "You oughta come to church some Sunday with me and Gwen. There's a single gent, Roland, who brings his mum and he's nice as can be. No slouch in the looks department, and he doesn't seem the sort to send a gal a picture of his genitals either."

"Thanks, but I'll pass." Dana covers her mouth, pushing a yawn back down her throat. "Give my best to Gwen and her harem."

Marge laughs, lifting her bulk out of the car. "Y'know, Gwen wouldn't mind giving it a whirl, age is just a number and all, but these yahoos only want one thing."

"If only," Dana mutters as Marge shuts the door, gives another little wave, and trundles up her walk.

That was the fundamental problem with Tinder and the like: misrepresentation. Casual encounters were never truly casual. Men would say no strings, yet Dana inevitably found herself snared in a web of their expectations. Then she discovered HOok. An app designed exclusively for spontaneous single encounters, anonymity encouraged, and once contact is initiated the app permanently blocks your hook-up after forty-eight hours. It's too perfect. Too easy.

She taps the steering wheel, vacillating. It's been a weird day. Ben and Ms. Partridge. Even slight deviations from routine have a way of making her think, or rethink. Sex three times a week is hardly pathological, but three different men is red flaggy, no three-ways about it. Like cheesecake and vodka, stranger-fucking is best enjoyed within set limits. She needs a night alone. To keep her body to herself, entertain the notion of shame, and wonder if she's capable of spinning her own web.

She puts the car in gear. Emotions were made to be eaten, and Dana knows just the place.

In an older suburb of mature trees, mid-century bungalows, and expensive infills on oversized lots, the mall is dying in spite of surrounding solvency. A consumerist cathedral, clinging to life through dreamers seduced by cheap rent only to close within months when grim reality hits. Rich or poor, people prefer to order their dross online. The only people the mall attracts are elderly power walkers, bin pickers looking for a better climate, and stoners with the munchies.

Dana sweeps down the wide knave, under darkened skylights, over gleaming beige floors, past garbage cans with ashtrays on top, empty but for the odd gum wrapper. Tucked away in the transept, the food court is no less a manifestation of purgatory than the rest of the place. Every bay shuttered except the Dairy Queen, with two inert drones behind the counter, and Wok-Wok, the greasy Chinese joint run by a Lebanese family.

"Long time," the patriarch says when she approaches the counter. "Chow mein and fried rice?"

"And a—"

"Spring roll," he says, lifting an old-school foam container off the tall stack.

She carries her sad-lady meal to one of the orange tables, and slides into an attached plastic seat. When Dana was a kid, her mom coming home with Chinese food meant bad news. It meant the end of something. Dana's mom was often sad.

The first bite is everything she wants: salty-sweet, oily, and just shy of mushy. *Comfort food, imp,* her mother would have said. *Next best thing to love.*

"D'you have any idea how much sodium is in that?"

She looks up. "Ben?"

He bites at the chocolate-dipped cone in his hand. "Almost didn't recognize you out of a lab coat."

"And I thought you were watching your blood sugar...and vegan."

"Life is for living, Dana." His funny smile shows that crooked tooth, and his eyes are lit up neon red.

No wonder he is so uncharacteristically chill. He's baked.

Dana slurps from her paper cup of iced tea, gesturing to the empty orange chair across. "Join me?"

Ben flops into the seat. Dana notices the Shoppers Drug Mart bag dangling from his fist. "Don't tell me you're seeing another pharmacist."

"Needed antifungal cream. It's over the counter and you'd just tell me I don't have ringworm."

"You don't."

"There ya go."

"How the hell would you contract ringworm?"

"You tell me, PharmD."

"Wise ass," she mumbles through a mouthful of spring roll.

"Y'know, there are less depressing places to get bad noodles."

"I like Wok-Wok." She waves at the gentleman behind the counter and he waves back. "They know me."

"'Course they do. We don't get a lot of normies here."

"Guess I've never gotten high and shambled to the mall, convinced I had ringworm."

"Anxiety, Dana. Cannabis is proven to alleviate symptoms in test subjects who are otherwise wound tight as fuck."

"Truly, I've never seen you this relaxed."

He drapes an arm over the back of the empty chair beside him. "I've never seen you at eye level."

"Changes everything."

He redirects his gaze to her steaming clamshell.

14

"Gonna finish that?"

"Yes." She shoves her food to the middle of the tacky table. "But I'll share, if you can stand the sodium."

The noodles are quick to go. The rice lasts longer. Ben rises from the table, thanks her for the grub, tells her to have an "awesome night," and wanders off into the desolate beige, moving in a looser version of his distinctive scuttle.

Dana finishes her drink, and gets up to leave. "Oh…"

Ben's traitorous purchase sits abandoned on the orange chair. She could leave it. Or throw it away. He's fine. He doesn't have ringworm. Why would someone pretend to be sick when they're not? Why would they take medication they didn't need? Why would they lie? Acid bubbles into her esophagus, alongside the memory of her exchange with Ms. Partridge.

Her phone buzzes in her pocket.

Dana snatches the bag and runs. Past a pair of shuffling olds in matching track suits, an H&R Block, a juice cleanse kiosk, a heavyset gentleman demo-ing a Millenium Falcon drone outside the last RadioShack in the known universe. She runs past miles of steel-gated store fronts.

Outside the mall entrance there's no sign of him. Only a sparsely occupied parking lot. The Shoppers Drug Mart bag hangs from her hand like dog droppings. She knows the pharmacist: Callum is competent, if brusque. It's only antifungal cream. Ben can get another tube. Or she can hang onto it; he said he'd drop by tomorrow. Or…she could give him a call; she has his number in her system. And his address.

"Do not do this," Dana mutters even as she pulls out her phone and opens her remote desktop app. Kidd, Benjamin lives only a few blocks away in Spruce Cliff. "He doesn't have ringworm."

I've got a feeling about this one, imp. Dana cringes, remembering the lilt of hope in her mother's voice. Always hopeful. Every time.

She drives slowly. Alongside the golf course, down wide streets, and wide lots. Lawns bulging with poplar roots, littered with patches of snow and the last leathery leaves of November. The house sits on a corner, a sprawling bungalow with stucco arches, brick pillars, and a big front door of dark wood. Not fancy but these old neighbourhoods are expensive. Does he live with his parents?

The bell rings, reverberating through the porch. Earthy air kisses Dana's cheeks as the door swings open, revealing a young woman. Frizzy hair, cropped pants, and bare feet. Foot, actually. The left clearly a prosthesis.

"Heya," she says, thumping her plastic toes, nails varnished red, on the welcome mat.

Dana reminds herself that she's on a professional errand. "Does Ben live here?"

The girl snaps her gum, making intense eye contact.

"Benny! Door!"

She grinds her Juicy Fruit between her molars, eyes unblinking. Dana loses the staring contest, dropping her gaze to her own feet, all ten phalanges wriggling in her shoes. The girl looks barely twenty. Sister? Girlfriend?

"Ben!" the girl shrieks, and the sound of socks striking hardwood heralds Ben, swinging around the corner, red eyes wide.

"Dana?"

"Dana?" the young woman asks, then blows a bubble that pops over her nose and mouth before her tongue reels the whole mess back in. "You're the chemist?"

"I tried calling," Dana lies, wondering why she didn't call. Who just shows up at a person's house? If Ben appeared at her door unannounced she'd mace him. She doesn't know what to say, so she reiterates the fiction, as if that makes it real. "I tried to call."

Ben squints. "Okay...why?"

Dana roots through her tote and pulls out the Shoppers bag, holding it aloft.

The girl elbows Ben. "Invite her in, you rude fucker."

"Mind your business hop-a-long," Ben says, not unkindly, and then turns back to Dana. "Wanna?"

Dana does. She wants to see how Ben lives. Wants to know about the strange girl. She slips off her loafers and follows him toward the rear of the house, where the humidity intensifies.

A botanical scent envelopes her as Ben leads her down into

16

a sunken den with an attached sunroom occupied by at least a hundred potted plants, trees, and vines.

"Your very own jungle," Dana remarks over the hiss of built-in misters.

"Hyperoxygenation," Ben says. "Filters toxins out of the air. Good for the lungs but you gotta watch for mould. I have a filter that's supposed to catch spores. Don't think it's working though."

"You can't get ringworm from plants." Their knuckles collide when she shoves the Shoppers bag into his hand. "This is your house?"

"House, office, asylum, and arboretum."

"Just you and your girlfriend?"

Ben nudges her arm with the bag. "Subtle, Dana."

She burrows her toes into the rug as Ben plucks a withered leaf off a fern.

"Louise isn't my girlfriend: I'm not woman enough for her tastes. She and Porky are my roommates, and they work for me."

"Who?"

"Francis when he's got his ears on. Our office is in the basement."

Dana can't imagine flatting with Marge and Gwen and wonders exactly what kind of "office" runs out of Ben's basement. "How did Louise lose her foot?"

"Childbirth."

"Having a baby, or when she was a baby?"

Ben shrugs. "No one knows."

He busies himself with the plants, inspecting and pruning, while explaining how he found his housemates in the mall. Louise, jailbreaking iPhones, and Porky trying to sell essential oils by giving free hand massages. Neither of those kiosks are there anymore.

"You keep the marijuana crop in the office?" Dana says, half joking.

"Naw." He leans further into the foliage. "No money in it, now that it's legal. Louise makes more off one of her videos than I could in a month of selling black-market weed."

"What kind of videos?"

He pulls his head out of a spider plant. "You always need to know so much about people you've just met?"

He makes a good point. What use is that information to her? Then again, why is he making her work for it? Why bring it up in the first place? What's in the basement? What is she doing here? Begging the questions. "I should go."

"You just got here."

"I can't stay." She backtracks out of the living room. "I...have to feed my cat."

His eyebrows knit. "You don't have a cat."

"I do so."

She does not. The closest she's come to pet ownership is a cloud of fruit flies from an overripe banana.

"I'm glad you don't," Ben says, following her to the door. "I'm wicked allergic to cats and asking a woman to leave her clothes on the front porch is awkward."

Dana tries to laugh.

"Come back tomorrow, Dana."

She doesn't get out much. She's invited in even less. This is Ben. *Ben.* With his indoor flora, human fauna, and basement industry. There's exactly one social situation she can expertly navigate, and this is definitely not it.

"I'll check my schedule."

"Just come."

She tightens her fist around her car keys. "Don't tell me what to do."

"Please?" He stares at the floor, carefully handling her fragility in this moment.

"Why?"

He locks eyes with her. "Because you're ready."

He's pushing too hard. He's not normal.

"Ready for what?" she asks.

"You did me a favour tonight." Ben touches his finger to her forehead, lightly twisting like a pestle into a mortar. "Maybe I can do something for you."

On the long drive home, his fingerprint burns on her forehead. Dana knows she's in trouble. *I have a feeling about this one...* But this is Ben, and he doesn't need antifungal cream any more than

18

Theodora Partridge needs Oxy. He collects broken things, and ready or not, he's seen her damage.

The next day, Dana doesn't check her schedule. She doesn't call either. *Just come*, he'd said. Dana isn't in the habit of taking orders from men. After work, she drives home, takes a shower, and stands naked in her kitchen eating a dinner of eggs on toast. She's restless.

She opens HOok and drops her line. Within minutes she has three bites. Before HOok, a certain amount of work was required to get in and out of the relationship. Just enough to regularly keep her celibate for weeks at a time. Now it's too easy. There's no thrill. After her bizarre encounter with Ben last night, she craves something taboo. She releases her bites and reels in her line.

An exterior entrance permits direct access to Shoppers Drug Mart, thus bypassing the temptation of going to Wok-Wok two nights in a row. Ingress without a ripple, her loafers glide along waxed linoleum. She peruses aisles, blue-white and hermetic as a biotech lab, punctuated by gold, black, and scarlet displays. Nothing like her tiny store, with its warped floors, mismatched wooden shelves, and natural light. Her non-medicinal inventory is limited to incontinence pads, baby formula, magazines, and the hypoallergenic skin care line she makes in-house. Half of Shoppers is cosmetics and hair products.

Dana fingers her own stock-photo blonde pharmacist bob. Time for a trim. Maybe she'll get the pixie her stylist swears is perfect for her face. Or grow it long. Or dye it red. This is the hook of Shoppers Drug Mart. Welcoming you in, telling you how great you look, *but don't you think you could be just a little better?* With a clunk, the store switches to half lighting. Classic closing strategy.

She strolls up to the dispensary. A caustic middle-aged man lurks in the back shelves. They're well acquainted through years of conference small talk. *Don't shit where you eat* briefly banners across her mental screen. She raps the counter. "Can I get some service, please? I swear these corporate chains have no soul."

He pushes his magnifiers back on his head, frowns, and slides them back on his nose. "Dana."

"Hello, Callum."

He turns back to his checklist. "Shouldn't you be conjuring your potions on the millennial side of town?"

"At this ungodly hour? They're at home swilling kombucha and binging Netflix. I close early."

"Well, I work for the man and I've got five minutes before heading home to a Coors Light, so if you don't mind."

"Waiting?" Dana asks. "Not at all. Beer sounds great."

Callum's grumpy face doesn't integrate well with his expression of surprise. This is what Dana needs. Familiar terrain with just a hint of the unknown. There's something to be said for old-school prowling.

"Not a purely social call," Dana says. "My best customer has been led astray. You might know him. Came in the other day for antifungal cream."

"Ringworm. I know him from way back. Used to fill his Adderall scripts. Guess he goes to you now. So, who's stealing customers from who?"

"He likes the vegan capsules."

Callum jots something down on his clipboard. Dana wonders why they aren't using digital inventory programs.

Ten minutes later, they're walking through the parking lot. To her surprise, he pulls her into the back of his roomy Chrysler to deliver what she'd thought she would have to wait until the bottom of a can of cheap beer for.

Callum fucks like a freight train, and Dana helps herself to an orgasm, coming with her face pressed into the seat, the gamey taste of leather in her mouth. Afterward there's no awkward sneaking out. No obligatory exchange of numbers. Just a brisk straightening of clothes. He mutters something about her being crazy and kisses her roughly on the forehead before they go their separate ways.

It's the best sex she's had in years.

Already she grieves the loss of it, the potential of what it could turn into.

What might it be like to let him hold her?

Dana is behind the dispensary, installing updates on their network, while Marge cashes out in the front.

"You gonna lock up, chickie?"

"For the last time, yes," Dana replies. "Be gone. You'll be late for bingo and I'll feel the wrath of Gwen for keeping you."

"Going stag tonight. Gwynnie's got a date."

"Who's the lucky dick pic?"

"Lord knows. I gave her a rape whistle and expect a proof-of-life call at eight." Marge hauls her purse onto her shoulder. "You're welcome to accompany me to bingo."

"The day I'm that desperate is the day I swallow the bottle of expired Vicodin in my medicine cabinet."

Twelve days since Wok-Wok and Ben. Eleven since Callum. She finds herself thinking of the latter more than the former. Callum the curmudgeon. She didn't know him well, but she genuinely liked him, and now she won't ever be able to look upon him without nausea. And all because she needed...something. These thoughts—she won't go as far as calling them regrets—have kept her at home and off HOok every evening since.

The door jingles. A broad woman in shapeless jeans enters the pharmacy and strides past Marge. Unhurried, but purposeful, like a rhinoceros.

"Ms. Partridge, hello," Dana says.

Partridge nods and slides a sheet of paper across the counter. "Can you fill this before you close, or should I come back?"

Dana picks up the form. "Your last Oxy-Neo prescription didn't have any refills."

"New prescription, obviously."

"And a new doctor."

"Regular doc is on vacation, this one is her..." Partridge snaps her thick fingers.

"Locum," Dana says. "And she prescribed more medication not even two weeks after you filled a thirty day supply?"

"Is that a problem?"

"It's...unusual."

Partridge maintains steady eye contact. "Are you going to fill it or what?"

Dana's jaw clenches. "Narcotics are in a time-locked safe. It won't open until tomorrow."

"I'll come back."

"It's not personal, Ms. Partridge."

"Why would I take it personally?"

Dana studies her customer. Face sagging, slightly reddened eyes, and dry lips. Could be the normal exhaustion of chronic pain. However, Partridge has a too-stillness about her, like a mask covering something animated. Something hungry. And all Dana can bring herself to say is, "I'll have to confirm this with the prescribing physician."

"Yeah, you do that." Partridge drums her fingers on the counter and glances at the diploma on the wall. "Dana."

On her way out, Partridge turns her brick of a body sideways, allowing room for Marge to bustle up to the counter. "What was that all about?" she whispers.

Dana unlocks her jaw and drops the script into the tray for tomorrow's orders. "It's nothing."

"Honey, you gotta learn to crab about rotten customers, or you'll explode."

"You sound like my mother."

Marge squints. "Sometimes I forget you didn't hatch from an abandoned egg."

"Well, thanks." Dana slouches onto the stool in front of the computer.

Marge squeezes her shoulder. "Sure you don't want to come to bingo?"

"I'm thinking of getting a cat."

Marge clucks her tongue. "That lonely life of yours. You could at least let Jesus under your lab coat."

"Marge, you dirty old lady."

"I mean church. Showed Roland your picture, the pretty one Gwen took of us at the lake."

"You showed a guy named *Roland*, a picture of me in a bathing suit?"

"You look darling in it."

"Jesus."

"Mary and Joseph," Marge trills. "You'd think he'd never seen a belly button before."

Dana scans her sexual Rolodex for a Roland and comes up blank. So blank that her next words emerge spontaneously, escaping before she can stop them. "Actually, I'm meeting a friend tonight."

"You don't have friends."

Dana winces. "I have you."

"Still, this is a new development. Anyone I know?"

Dana hits okay on the last software update. "Um...it's Ben."

"Ben." Marge blinks behind her bifocals. "Our Ben? Pandora's Box Ben?"

"We ran into each other at the mall a while back. Got to talking. He asked me to drop by."

"Oh, Dana..." Marge trails off, searching for words, or perhaps tact. "Well, he's awful young."

"Only fourteen years—oh god, I know..." Dana shuts her eyes. "But we're not dating or anything, we just...get along."

"Say no more, chickie," Marge says with a cackle. "'Long as he's not sending you pictures of his genitals."

"So far, so good."

But is it? She and Ben never formally exchanged numbers, and he hasn't been in the store. Perhaps he's miffed that she stood him up. She could call, but what would she say? Sorry, I lied about having a cat? Sorry that, instead of coming over to your house the next night, I had sex with the pharmacist you'd cheated on me with for your imaginary ringworm? Sorry, I have no idea how to function as a social animal outside certain narrow parameters and I can't stop thinking about what you do in your basement?

She's still thinking when she steps onto his front porch and pushes the glowing orange bell.

Louise opens the door mid-yawn. Blue toenails today. "Benny's in the basement, c'mon."

Dana follows Louise as she thumps across the living room with its seventies-era stone and macramé accents, and chlorophyll aroma. On their first meeting, Dana catalogued Louise according to her physical flaws and now wonders how she failed to notice the girl's perfectly turned limbs, and the way her rounded hips sway in her yoga capris. When Louise twists to open the basement door, her breasts shift under her t-shirt, high, full, and braless.

"Take a picture," Louise says.

Dana blinks. "I...I'm sorry."

"Naw, go ahead." Louise thrusts out her chest. "Sometimes when God takes a foot, he gives you incredible tits."

Dana pulls her cardigan closed over her comparatively sexless architecture. She hears Ben's lightly congested coughing below.

"You're cool, right?" Louise points down the stairs. "Benny trusts his gut, but me, I gotta hear it from your mouth. And since I know you're still wondering, it's not like that between us."

"Is he gay?" Dana asks, thinking that, if Louise is, it would make sense.

"Dunno." Louise fiddles with a frizzy curl. "He's not like...a sexual person."

Ben appears at the bottom of the stairs, holding a cardboard box. "You know I can hear you."

"Like I care?" Louise retorts.

Without actually looking at Dana, Ben asks, "How's your cat?"

"Well fed," Dana says, and nods to Louise. "I'm cool."

Ben clears his throat and beckons. "Come on down, PharmD."

A thrill races along the arches of her feet with each descending stair. They could be into anything.

Heroin, Nazi gold, human trafficking. The last thing she expects is a stocky man standing at a workbench, his back to her, lightly fuzzed buttocks peeking from under the hem of a white t-shirt.

24

"Oh." Dana drops her gaze to the shag carpet.

"Jeez, Benny, you didn't tell her?" Louise flicks his ear.

"Ow... Thought you would've."

Dana reaches for the stair rail. "I think I should go."

"Wait." Ben's rough hand clutches her wrist. "Porky's not a pervert. He just likes to be free, y'know?"

"A nudist?"

"Naturist if he's got his ears on, but yeah."

"Wears a shirt cuz he's self-conscious about his gut," Louise added. "That's why we call him Porky, like the pig."

Offended on Porky's behalf, Dana wonders what they call her behind her back. Then Porky, having sensed the commotion behind him, turns to face the room while fitting an ancient set of bulky beige hearing aids over his ears. Dana attempts to train her gaze somewhere that allows only the faintest peripheral glimpse of his genitals, a word she can't think without hearing it in Marge's voice.

"You came back." His consonants flatten in the manner of the profoundly hearing impaired, but he's otherwise perfectly intelligible.

Ben slaps Porky on the shoulder. "Francis here does web maintenance, order processing, and customer support. Lou's product management, anything metal-facing."

"Metal?"

"Lead. The batteries people use to prop up their networks during a power outage. We sell refurbished units on the internet."

Dana scans the rest of the room and notes a rack of industrial shelving loaded with batteries. Some contained in branded plastic housing, some not.

"Refurbished," she says. "You mean counterfeit?"

"Off-brand units that don't pass factory QA, but Lou makes sure they check out before we slap a top shelf label on 'em and ship. At a fraction of the price, customer gets what they're paying for." Ben says it matter-of-factly as though these are fundamental criteria of any legit form of commerce.

A peg board hung with an array of tools lines the wall, and on either side of the workbench is a desk with a computer. There's racks of batteries and another shelving unit with what appears to be typical basement detritus. Cans of paint, lightbulbs, a VCR, boxes labelled "Christmas," "Camping," and "72-hour Emergency." No meth lab, no dog fighting ring.

Dana tries to muster some disapproval but curiosity wins out. "And what's your role?"

Ben shrugs. "Same as any B-school grad. Strategy."

"You don't seem the MBA type."

"Because I'm not an analyst in a cube farm, or the CEO of an artisanal hair wreath start-up?" He meets her eyes for the first time since coming downstairs. "I learned more about projections, procurement, and marketing selling dime bags than I did in any lecture hall."

Dana can't help laughing. "So, you were a drug dealer?"

"Problem solver," Ben says, rubbing his palms together, his voice and posture energized in a way she's never seen. "I dealt in solutions. An herbal relaxation inducement without the side effect of munchies. Hired an Estonian kid over the net to develop an app, had a few campus burnouts beta test, and it went viral. I couldn't keep up."

Louise smirks. "He called it Baked Not Fried."

Dana's chemist brain lights up. "You laced it with something?"

"Adderall." Ben nods. "Vape it all together. Cannabis fucks you up."

"While the amphetamine suppresses appetite. That's brilliant—" Dana frowns. "Where did you get the Adderall?"

His eyes dart wall to wall and he shoves his hands in his pockets.

At first Dana doesn't understand, then her stomach sinks like it's full of cement. "Of all your bullshit afflictions, that's the one I actually believed."

"I've got anxiety," Ben says. "Last thing you wanna give me is speed."

The big picture snaps into focus. Shortly after she took over the space, previously (and ironically) a head shop, and opened the pharmacy, Ben was one of her first customers. She found herself filling dozens of monthly Adderall prescriptions, mostly for children, but a fair number for students. College town and all. More than once she'd spent an evening in those narrow dorm beds. Her face heats and her throat feels swollen.

"How many phony scripts went through my pharmacy?"

"All legit. They're easy to get—"

Her dry tongue rasps out the words, "You used me."

"You were the only place in town that kept the immediate release stuff on hand."

Ben did his homework. Cased her. Knew that as a compounding chemist she kept a lot of unformulated basics in stock. Her entire body shudders. "I don't care about your battery scam, but I have professional ethics."

"Nothing I did can ever blow back on you, I promise. I shut it all down over two years ago."

"Except I still fill that script for you, every month."

Ben swallows and just then his thyroid does look enlarged. "I don't sell. But it greases the wheels when I need to...negotiate."

"Were you ever my friend?" The words taste burnt as they drop out of her mouth. Now she sounds like her mother.

"What? Yeah...yes, of course."

He's lying. He's been lying to her all along.

"Then I'm confused, because I don't lie to my friends." Or she wouldn't, if she had them. "I don't trick them into doing bad things."

This isn't about Ben. Not entirely. But she won't be pushed into compliance. She rolls her shoulders back and nails him with direct eye contact. "Have I got it wrong then?"

"Dana, come on."

"Oh, sorry. Am I making you uncomfortable? Should I smile and tell you it's fine that your college experiment could have ruined my life?"

"You're overreacting."

Flames leap up her throat and scorch her teeth.

What an idiot she is, thinking she could have something so novel as a friend. She and Ben aren't friends. They're barely acquaintances. She's outraged, but more than that, it hurts. Badly.

Because it's every boyfriend who shattered her mom's heart, leaving Dana to cut herself on the pieces. It's Ms. Partridge and her fake back pain. Doctor shopping. Lying to her face. Not caring that Dana could lose her licence. Not caring that Dana's business is all she has because no one has ever cared about her, only what they could get from her. But the boyfriends aren't here. Her mom isn't here. Partridge isn't here. Ben is here. And he did the worst thing of all. He gave her hope.

Louise's chin drops to her chest and Porky rubs her shoulder. Ben's hands jam deeper into his pockets. His jaw tics as though he wants to say something but can't find his words.

"I'm leaving," Dana says, voice shaking. "Don't follow me, and don't contact me again."

She runs up the stairs, spills into the living room, and trips over the area rug. Before she can break her fall, her kneecap strikes the corner of the stone hearth with a hollow crack. A neon beam lasers up her femur and into her pelvis, where it settles in a cloudy puddle of nausea.

She groans into the shag rug. An attempt to move her leg produces a wet squish of agony, and bile surges into her esophagus. A satin-finish foot thumps down in front of her face.

"Christ on a spear."

Dana hears Louise but can't see much outside of the pain kaleidoscope.

"Up you get."

Hands hook under Dana's armpits and Juicy Fruit wafts over her face. She cries out sharply as she's hoisted onto the couch.

"Breathe, okay?" Louise wiggles a cushion under Dana's leg until it's positioned at a tolerable degree of flexion. "You're all right, just breathe. And don't look."

Dana looks, and gags. Beneath her torn leggings a swollen red-black gash bleeds freely down her shin. The pain gives way to shock, as endorphins flood her vascular system.

Louise bangs her prosthesis on the floor three times. Porky emerges from the basement, a grimace smeared across his face.

"First aid kit," he blats and flees across the living room, his exposed bottom twitching as he vanishes down the hallway. Dana is grateful to be spared a frontal view of Porky's hustle.

"God, I don't belong here," she moans. "I need to go."

"You're not going anywhere, except maybe urgent care," Louise says.

Porky returns with a large plastic box, which Louise cracks open, revealing a first responder's array of supplies. Louise pulls the cardboard sheath off a scalpel. "I'm gonna have to cut that off."

"What?" Dana lurches and whinnies. Porky covers his face and races back down the basement stairs.

"The leggings. Like we're cannibals or something?" Louise goes to the liquor cabinet, pours three fingers of whiskey into a tumbler, and shoves it into Dana's hand along with two extra-strength Tylenol. "Drink up, sis."

At this point Dana doesn't know which way is up, so she sinks into the cushions, chases her pills with alcohol, and lets Louise cut her pants off. The girl is swift if not overly gentle, and soon Dana's knee is clean and swaddled with gauze.

"Thanks, Lou," Dana hears herself say through a dreamy haze. "Sorry to be so much trouble."

"You gotta get a lid on yourself." Louise fastens the last piece of tape. "Porky is an empath. He literally feels your pain, and you know what Ben is like out in the world. He's probably losing his mind down there. This house is his sanctuary, and you just bled all over it."

"Not my finest moment," Dana mutters into her empty glass.

"His own fault, that blabbermouth." Louise glares at the basement door. "I ought to kick his ass."

"You've only got one foot."

"I'll kick yours too, bitch." She pulls out her phone. "You can't drive. I'm getting you an Uber. Amir can be here in ten minutes."

"Blue Civic?"

"Yeah."

"No good," Dana says. She often concludes wine-drunk HOok encounters with an Uber to the mall and Wok-Wok. And sometimes that led to a nightcap. "He and I...um, well..."

"Serious?" Louise's expression is half incredulity, half admiration. "Okay, what about Neil in a black Mini Cooper?"

"No."

"You fuck him too?"

"I've never fucked anyone named Neil and I'd like to keep it that way."

"Okay, what about Bjorn?"

Dana groans and pats the pocket of her cardigan, finding it empty. "I lost my phone."

Louise picks it up off the floor beside the fireplace. "Cracked your screen pretty good. Still works though."

"Damn it. Should be an app on there for another ride service I use."

Louise scrolls through and laughs. "Boober?"

"Yeah, it's a 'by women, for women' kind of thing."

"Don't mind the sound of that," Louise chuckles and shakes her head. "Ride'll be here in fifteen. Can I safely assume you don't know Katie or her silver Acura in the biblical sense?"

"I'm heterosexual."

"You're a slut."

"Beg your pardon?" Dana hopes her face is making the right expression: one of open-mouthed confusion and not shifty-eyed guilt.

"Straighty one-eighty or not, I knew there was something off about you." Louise flops down on the couch next to her. "This tabernacle of freaks; normies can't cross the threshold."

Dana considers this, lightly biting the rim of her glass. "Does seem that way."

"Hell yeah." Louise seizes Dana's limp flipper of a hand and high-fives it. "Variety is the spice of weird. If you're looking for a scolding, you've got the wrong house. And I think you belong here."

"Why?"

"Because you *are* here." Louise grabs the whiskey bottle and refills Dana's glass. "Life is about finding your people, Dana. We're all looking for our gang, even if we don't know it. It's like, the most important thing."

"Thank you, Louise," Dana says, curiously wanting to hug the girl who doesn't seem so much like a girl anymore.

Louise stands, dubiously surveying her work. "Promise you'll get that looked at? By a professional?"

Dana waves her off. "If I lose the leg I'll move in, join the circus."

"Be nice to have another girl around."

"I'll make amputee porn," Dana slurs. "Could you teach me?"

Louise scowls. "He told you about my videos?"

"Mentioned it."

"I'm gonna staple his gob shut. It's not porn, it's YouTube, for Christ's sake."

This is private property, but Dana can't seem to stay off the grass. "As if your clicks aren't mostly from perverts."

"Oh, fuck you," Louise says, disdain dripping from her turned-down mouth. "Some are foot guys, sure. But there's also other gimps, and kids born without this or that, and it doesn't goddamn well matter who or what they are because for three minutes they get to feel okay about it."

Dana swallows the last of her whiskey. "I misunderstood."

"Yeah, you fucking did. Not everything is about sex, so maybe try not thinking with your button for a change." Louise slaps the side of Dana's knee.

"Ow..."

"Have a nice life." She stomps out of the living room and down the hall, where a door opens and closes with a terrific bang.

The Boober is still ten minutes away. Ten minutes in a house where she's no longer welcome. Dana's gathering the courage to drag herself to the front door when footsteps thud up the basement stairs. She braces herself to deal with Ben, but it's Porky who emerges, a curl in his front tail and a furrow in his forehead.

"Impressive," he says. "You managed to run Louise off, and Ben is so shut down he's practically comatose."

"I'm sorry, Francis—" Dana's voice catches in horror as tears spill down her face. "This has been a very strange night."

Porky crosses the living room to the massive planter and tears out a few sprigs. He rubs them briskly between his hands then brushes them back into the planter. The scent of lavender wafts through the room. He pulls the stopper on a bottle of oil, dripping a small amount into his palm. Kneeling at her feet, he takes her hand. His heat burns into her cold skin, thumbs tracing the lines of love, life, and fate, travelling along the nerve paths and across muscle fibres, from wrist to fingertip.

Dana wants to explain, get Porky on her side. Ben betrayed her. Why would he ask her to come here? As she relaxes into Porky's touch, she realizes now isn't the time for building alliances or asking questions. The massage is as much for Porky's benefit as it is hers.

Besides, the answers are all around.

Porky and Lou. Lonely. Struggling. Strange. Ben found them. Just like he'd found her.

An arrival notification flashes on her screen. Porky snags a robe off the back of the armchair and slips it on. Then he helps her out the door and into Katie's Acura. On the way home, an unnerved Katie repeatedly asks if she wouldn't rather go to the hospital, then insists on helping her up the steps to her condo. Dana experiences a flash forward, imagining herself as an old woman supported by the competent grip of her young care worker.

Once inside, Dana showers Katie with five stars and a ridiculous tip. Then she hobbles to the bathroom, dry swallows two of the expired Vicodin, and slides into bed, plummeting into sleep on a whiff of lavender.

Care, precision, and opiates are not the coziest of cellmates, so after a trip to Urgent Care, it's another two days before she's able to drag herself into the shower, call another Boober—Katie, again—and return to work, albeit on crutches with an open patellar fracture. By lunchtime, Marge finally gets the hint that Dana doesn't want to discuss the matter or be fussed over. Of course, that doesn't stop every well-intentioned customer from inquiring.

"What happened to you?"

Dana reaches for her crutches and turns toward the counter

where the second-last person she wants to see ever again is standing.

"Ms. Partridge."

Partridge gestures to the bulky brace swaddling Dana's leg. "Looks like you did a number on yourself."

Dana bristles. "Can I help you?"

Patridge doesn't smile but her eyes crinkle with amusement. "Here to pick up the prescription I brought in the other day."

"The Oxy-Neo," Dana says flatly.

"And diclofenac." Partridge nods toward the pick-up basket. "Should be there. Your fill-in person said it would be ready today... you sure you're okay?"

Partridge's concern almost sounds sincere, but Dana never said she *was* okay in the first place. Her knee is on fire, her mouth tastes like metal, and she just wants to get through this day so she can go home and swallow her own prescription narcotics. In this moment, she would gladly hand Partridge a wheelbarrow of hydromorphone to go away. Instead, she rings the prescription through.

"You'll want to avoid taking NSAIDS, ibuprofen, or naproxen, in conjunction with the topical diclofenac cream," she advises, handing over the bag and wincing when her leg accidentally bumps the shelf under the counter.

"That's gotta hurt." Partridge pivots on an enormous Doc Marten and saunters to the door, pausing to call back over her shoulder. "Might want to try this diclofenac stuff. I hear it's a great alternative."

Several pain-blurred hours later, the clock finally creeps toward closing. Dana is exhausted, sweaty, and gritting her teeth against the relentless throb of her leg. She pulls out her shattered phone to book a ride home when Ben scampers through the front door. Twitchy and bright-eyed as a squirrel.

"Hello, stranger," Marge sings in a knowing tone that crawls over Dana's skin. Ben makes a beeline for her platform.

As though sensing her intention to deny him an audience, he pulls his hand out of his pocket and places her car key on the counter.

"Do you even have a driver's licence?" Dana asks.

"Figured you would have picked it up by now. I was worried."

"I told you to leave me alone." She speaks in a low voice, thwarting

Marge's attempt to eavesdrop.

"Can't we talk about this?"

"About how you're a liar, and a fraud?"

"For starters, yeah." Ben holds his arms out. "But I know you got more, so lay it on me."

"You cultivated a relationship with me under false pretences and kept it up for years. I'd suggest you might be a psychopath if I didn't think it would delight you so much."

Ben reaches into his satchel and retrieves a white box. "Peace offering." He slides an iPhone across the counter.

"You didn't."

"Figure I owe you an upgrade, at the very least."

Dana pushes the box back. "Trying to buy me off?"

"You're not gonna narc on me." His shaking hands dive back into his pockets. "It's not a bribe. It's just... I wanted to do something good. Because what I did. It was a shitty thing."

"Quite." The word comes out so hard it threatens to chip her teeth.

He paces back and forth between end caps displaying fleet enemas and compression socks. His feet scuff along the floor, and his breath is shallow and uneven.

Dana sighs, letting her shoulders droop. "Please stop. My patella is fractured, I've been *Lost Weekending* on painkillers, and I can't do this right now."

"I'm not that guy anymore." He halts and nudges the phone back toward her. "Give me a chance to prove it."

Leaning on a crutch, she picks up the box and cradles it to her chest. "Benjamin, do you know what the most important part of a sincere apology is?"

He shakes his head.

"The words *I'm sorry.*"

He ducks his head, coughing into his elbow. "Okay, Mom."

"*Mom?*" She drops the phone back on the counter. "Why would you say something so creepy to me?"

"You're a little creepy yourself, PharmD." He coughs into his sleeve some more and pulls his inhaler out, puffing twice.

"Most of that is hitting the back of your throat."

"Spacer's at home."

"I've got some here."

"They aren't sterilized."

"You're a hypochondriac, not a germophobe." She rustles around in the back shelves, then returns with a disposable spacer. "These are left over from when I had the respiratory techs in doing pulmonary function tests. Meant to be used right out of the box."

"Uh-uh." Ben shies away, audibly wheezing. "I got pneumonia once from aspirating cardboard dust."

Dana grinds her knuckles into her forehead. "Jesus Christ, you would actually have asthma."

"You're salty today."

"Shut up," she snaps and then calls out to the front of the house. "Marge, are you okay closing? I'm going to drive this one home."

Grinning, Marge peeks out from behind the nearest shelf where she'd clearly been spying. "Don't do anything I wouldn't."

"Got a list?" Ben grunts, still coughing.

Dana pinches his arm.

"What, I'm kidding," he whispers.

"Another word, and I leave you to die." She grabs her coat, shoves the phone and the spacer in her bag, and saddles up on her crutches. Together, they shamble past a gleeful Marge, and out the door to where her car is parked on the street, climbing inside.

Ben coughs and rattles all the way.

"Just use the damn spacer," Dana says, pulling out into traffic, relieved that it's not her driving knee that's broken.

"I'm all right," he laughs. "Can I ask you a question?"

"You can ask."

"Why does Marge think we're...you know?"

"I told her we ran into each other and she got the wrong idea."

"Did she?" Ben asks, hand knotted around his inhaler, knuckles bleaching through the skin.

"Well, I didn't fall on my head, Ben. I think I'd remember fucking you."

"See? Salty," he wheezes. "Do you tell Marge everything?"

"She's my friend."

"Really?"

Dana fixes her eyes on the yellow light ahead. "We go on picnics at the lake. She invited me to church. To bingo. If that's not a friend, what is?

"She works for you."

"You live with your employees." She brakes faster than she means to, flinging them forward hard enough to lock their seatbelts.

"We're not exactly normal," Ben says, shakily loosening his shoulder strap. "And neither are you."

"What's that supposed to mean?"

"Church with Marge? You talk about friendship like it's something you read about in a book."

Dana pulls up to Ben's house, flips on the wipers and sprays the windshield, though there's no reason to do so. "Thanks for bringing my car back."

"Thanks for hiding your extra key in the most obvious spot." Ben shifts the car into park for her. "You should come in."

Dana grunts. "So we can talk about how broken and friendless I am?"

"We can talk about anything you want. Maybe the real reason you're so pissed? Not that you don't have a right to it, but I got a feeling there's more to the story."

Maybe he's right. Maybe it's Theodora Partridge, picking up her fresh refill of Oxy today, thumbs through her denim belt loops like she never doubted the outcome. Maybe it's Marge, her only real friend. Maybe it's Dana's mother, sweeping Dana's hair off her face, *I'd tell you to smile, imp, if it wouldn't break your face open.* Maybe, but these are things Dana doesn't talk about. She doesn't know how.

On her crutches, Dana follows Ben up to the porch and into the house. He leads her down into the living room, past the earthy warmth of the planter, to the open basement door.

"I'm home," he calls down.

"I'll alert the media," Louise yells up, then in a muffled growl says, "That knobweed just killed Templeton..."

"Not before we got our key word," Porky's flat voice replies.

36

"She here?" Louise yells again.

"Yep," Ben says.

"She okay? Both feet on the ground, head up her ass?"

Ben gives Dana a helpless shrug and calls back down, "Situation normal."

"She's okay," they hear Louise tell Porky. "Shit, the egg sac."

"Moving sac to Wilbur's mouth," says Porky, followed by a frantic clacking of keys.

Ben closes the basement door, coughing more thickly than in the car. "Every Sunday night, they get on the dark net with their online nerd herd and play text adventure games based on kid's books."

A sudden cold sweat leaks from Dana's pores as she backs away. Her whole leg throbs, her arms ache from being on crutches all day, and her lungs feel crumpled and stiff. "They hate me."

"It's a big house, PharmD. We can stay out of their way." His eyes narrow as he looks her over. "You're hurting."

Dana nods, glancing around at the orange couch, the wood panelling, the fireplace, and the massive planter. She is hurting. Bruised like a dropped apple. "Show me your room."

"My room?"

"I need to get off my feet, and I want to see your room."

His face darkens. "Search for contraband?"

"Cigarettes, moonshine." She adjusts the crutches under her armpits. "Coolers packed with kidneys."

"You watch too much TV."

"I also read a lot."

"Fine." His head sinks between his shoulders and she limps after him down the hall to the master bedroom. "Here it is."

Dana notes the lustre on every dust free surface and the herbal smell from two large potted ferns, an assortment of succulents lining the window ledge, and a few exotic flowering plants on his dresser.

She enters the room and touches a feathery white blossom. "Beautiful."

"Egret orchid," Ben says, reaching with both hands before jamming them back in his jacket pockets. "She doesn't like to be touched."

"Is that a waterbed?"

"No pressure points."

The bed is neatly made, with a pile of shipping labels, a box of counterfeit brand stickers, and a roll of packing tape scattered across the duvet. Dana notes the lack of a desk in the large room, or television, or computer, but he does have a bookcase loaded with hardcover reference books on horticulture and botany.

"You like plants."

"Most of those books are my mom's." Ben opens the closet, revealing empty hangers, some sweaters and coats, what appears to be a life jacket, and a few file boxes. "See? No smuggled ivory."

"What's in the boxes? Porn?"

"In a box?"

"I keep forgetting how young you are."

"If you wanna rifle through twenty years of *Spiderman*, be my guest."

Beside the boxes of comics and the floatation device, Dana spots an oxygen tank fitted with a regulator. Clear tubing runs from the tank to a face mask with a small nebulizer attached. "You really do have asthma."

"And pancreatic insufficiency." Ben shuts the closet with a snap. "Satisfied? Or do you think I'm selling my enzyme pills on the black market too?"

She eases herself down on the bed, setting off a wave dampened by the fibre-fill baffling. Ben paces between the closet and the bedroom door with his huddled gait, as if attempting to both run and hide at the same time. He is lanky, but not malnourished and certainly not jaundiced. His pancreas is probably fine.

"Makes you anxious, me being here," she says.

"Isn't that the idea?" He picks up speed, crossing the floor in front of her several more times. "Payback?"

"I want to know if I'm still being lied to. And," she gestures to the room as a whole, "the seventies serial killer motif isn't helping."

"What did you expect?"

"Dirty clothes on the floor. Video game consoles. A bong. Not mall ferns and a waterbed."

"Dana... I don't smoke because I have asthma, screens in the bedroom is bad for your sleep hygiene, and I put my laundry away because I'm a goddamn grown-up."

She snags his sleeve, meaning only to halt him, but he spins off balance, and the mattress heaves as she falls back onto the box of stickers with Ben on top of her.

He scrambles, rolling to the side and pulling her off the pokey boxes. "Your leg, are you okay?"

"Are you apologizing?"

"Not yet."

She brushes her knuckles over his scruffy jaw. "But you're thinking about it."

"Maybe." He grasps her forearm, thumb pressed against the inside of her wrist, their pulses banging together. "Truce?"

She nods.

At first his mouth barely brushes hers. Dana is wary. Most men are utterly terrible at kissing. So much that she avoids this oral activity whenever possible. The moisture levels, the crushing pressure, the race to cram the greatest length of tongue muscle down her esophagus as aggressively as possible. Ben is not aggressive. He's not passive. He's deliberate.

Minutes pass this way and it's only when the tip of Ben's tongue finds hers that she notices its complete absence thus far. He tastes like throat lozenges and smells like Static Guard—at least, the smell she associates with being a little girl and watching her mom get ready on date night: sipping warm chardonnay, lifting her skirt and spraying her nylons with the blue aerosol can, the corrosive flavour sticking to the back of Dana's throat. *I've got a feeling about this one, imp.*

Ben's kiss goes no further than the lightest sweep of his tongue over hers. An ache builds in her joints, a need to arch and flex. A craving more urgent than mere genital (damn Marge) contact. Dana's spine stretches, bowing up into a long crescent. Seeking.

Holding himself just out of reach, Ben pins her wrists to the bed on either side of her head. Grip firm. Mouth slow.

Dana has never been not-touched like this. Deliberately.

Then his mouth slides off hers and down her neck. He's gasping for air, sweating more than he should be. His breath turns metallic, rattling like a broken machine.

"Ben?"

Between wet coughs, he rolls off the bed and disappears into the hallway. Another door slams, and a tap hisses.

Dana closes her eyes, each breath flowing easy as she pictures gentle eddies swirling through dark water in the vinyl bag contouring to her body. This turn of events is unexpected and unsurprising. It's Ben. It's her. What did she think would happen?

After a time, there's a soft snick of a door closing and a wave of displaced mattress water. She opens her eyes as he settles beside her, letting her silence do the asking.

"I'm fine now," he says.

"You're the colour of a government building."

"Nothing to do with you." A weary half smile. "My lungs, my anxiety, it's a condition. I can't do...that stuff."

She rests her hand on his chest, feeling the rabbit rhythm beneath. "Louise says you're not a sexual person."

"Would you be, if you had to take beta blockers just to rub one out?"

Dana bites the insides of her cheeks.

He scowls. "Don't you dare laugh."

"If it makes you feel better, I've got my own issues."

"Lou says you like to put it about."

"Yes." Dana owns it with—not pride, but trending less toward shame. "It's more complicated than that."

"Tell me"

"Not sure I want to."

"Think you can scare me?"

She stares at the ceiling, popcorn style with glittering specks, and wonders if they're meant to stand in for stars. "I've never been with the same person more than once."

"Never?"

"I hook up with a guy, and the second it's over, I've got a whirlpool in my gut and ants under my skin. It's all I can do to get out the

40

door with my clothes on."

Ben's faintly cyanotic lips drop open. "Jesus, that's bent."

"See, you are scared."

"I'm not—would you have stopped? Would you have told me?"

"What do you mean?"

"I mean if my sympathetic nervous system hadn't flipped out, by now I'd be another repulsive memory you couldn't run away from fast enough. What are the ethics of that, PharmD?"

"Are you judging me?" She heaves herself to an awkward sitting position. "You're a criminal."

"Then why'd you kiss me?"

"You kissed me first." She cringes at the childish shrill of her voice.

"You're here for a reason. What do you think it is?"

Her knee twists against the brace as she attempts to stand. A blade of pain cuts deep and she pleats into herself, cry caught on her vocal cords like a kite in a tree.

Ben is similarly silent. Waiting. She fixes her gaze on the faulty stars in the ceiling. "No one wishes I were normal more than I do."

His fingers crawl over hers. "How do we do this?"

She squeezes his hand and dredges herself out of his bed. "We don't."

"Dana," he calls after her, but she's already on her crutches, thump-hopping out the door.

Marimba music teases her eyes open and she stares at the expanse of her own ceiling. Flat, featureless, no stars. She had the condo painted last year. The colour is Farrow & Ball, oyster shell. Different than white. Heightened dimension, said the saleslady. From this perspective, it does seem fathomless. For a moment, staring at that ceiling, the entire concept of Monday is sucked down her neural funnel like the last sluice of dirty dishwater.

And she's left with no choice but to reinvent.

The pharmacy is closed on Mondays. It's Dana's habit to go in anyway, on account of chores neglected during business hours, and also having no other earthly thing to do.

"I'm taking the day off," she announces to her bottomless ceiling and throws off the duvet.

Second thoughts strike in the shower, humid heat being their preferred habitat. Maybe just half a day. There are things to be done, but she could still knock off early and come home to...nothing. Any ordering can go through the apps on her phone. The dust will still be there tomorrow. Any physical item she might need, she already has at home. Dana realizes this impulse to take the day off is perhaps not as impulsive as it felt staring at the ceiling. She has no reason to work. No reason to stay home either.

"Should I get a cat?" she queries her reflection, giving her hair one last shot with the blow dryer.

Don't be Louise, don't be Louise, don't be Louise... Dana thinks as she hobbles up the front porch and cants forward on her crutches to ring the bell. Louise opens the door before Dana's finger touches the button.

"Saw you coming," Louise says, barefoot, a wedge of Juicy Fruit pushing her cheek out. "Benny's not here. Specialist appointment."

"What for?"

"Dunno, he sees like five different ones. Pulmonologist, cardiologist, dermatologist maybe? Seems pretty hung up on the ringworms."

"Not actually a worm."

"And he doesn't actually have it. Are we paying to heat the neighbourhood or what?" Louise steps aside.

Dana awkwardly flicks off her shoes, barely able to keep up with Louise as she trots down the hall, past Ben's fern gully, and

42

down again to the basement. Her crutches drum loudly on the thin carpeted steps. The workbench and desk are unoccupied.

"Where's Francis?" Dana gulps, trying to appear less completely out of breath than she is.

"His group does stuff on Monday afternoons." Louise flops down on a sofa too respectable-looking to reside in a basement. "They're at a movie, I think."

"Nudist movie screening?"

"Close captioned," Louise says. "For the hearing impaired, so you can release your pearls before you strangle yourself with 'em."

"I didn't mean anything—"

"Whatever, I saw that look on your face."

"What look?" She doesn't recall having a look. She didn't... Did she?

"Porky's rectum is cleaner than your mouth, slut."

Dana leans back on her crutches. "That...is incorrect."

"Why don't you limp your prissy ass out of our house. And I'll tell Benny you dropped by."

The ricochet between shame, anger, and confusion tips her equilibrium, and when she steps back, her crutch bangs against the bottom stair. With a jolt, she catches herself on the railing, and regains grip on her reason for being here. "Louise, I came to say I'm sorry, for the other night." She doesn't add that she had absolutely nothing else to do.

"This is an apology?" Louise crosses her arms under her pert breasts. "What fucking planet are you from?"

Dana fishes a brightly wrapped package out of her bag. "I brought you a present."

Louise lunges from the sofa and examines the package like a suspicious cat before swiping it from Dana's hand and flopping back down on the cushions. "You're still an asshole." She unwraps the bottle of clear nail polish and raises an eyebrow. "Even you ought to have more imagination than this."

"Mica." Dana lowers herself onto the couch next to Louise. "Ground ultrafine. Should be stable, but you might want to give it a shake. Under black light it shimmers like the aurora borealis.

I thought it would be interesting for your videos."

"So now you're okay with my foot porn?"

Dana has actually watched several of Louise's remarkably unremarkable videos. Fifteen-minute close-ups of her feet and toes, and sometimes her hands painting her toenails. She has over a half a million subscribers.

"I made assumptions," Dana says. "About both you and Frances. I treated you rudely in your own home. And I'm sorry."

"What about Benny?"

Dana pauses, and controls her face, not wanting to get yelled at again. "That conversation is more complicated."

Louise leans in and brushes a sweaty lock of hair off Dana's forehead. "I don't blame you for giving him shit. But that Baked business was a goldmine and he gave it up because he didn't feel right using you."

The basement door opens above them. "Lou? Is Dana down there?"

"Yeah," Louise shouts back. "We're talking about periods and witchcraft. Go away."

Ben descends halfway, fingers drumming along the railing. "Dana?"

Dana is glad to see him. At the moment, however, she's making headway with Louise and doesn't want any interference. "Wouldn't happen to have a black light would you?"

He points to the shelving unit beside Porky's desk. "Fire extinguisher is there too. Y'know, if you need it."

"Appreciated," Dana says and flicks her hand. "Now, be gone."

Once the basement door shuts, Louise reclines and slides her bare feet into Dana's lap. Dana stiffens, then holds her breath until her limbic system gives way to the vagus nerve's chillout signal. In this house, the rules of social engagement are different. Physical touch is doled out in a generously casual manner, without the weight of expectation. Dana could tell Louise this makes her uncomfortable and Louise would no doubt back off.

But *is* she uncomfortable?

"Well?" Louise wiggles one set of toes. "Let's do it."

Dana paints Louise's toenails black and then layers the clear polish overtop.

"Your turn. C'mere, sis." Louise grabs Dana's ankles, ignoring her wince, and wrestles her socks off to give her the same paint job.

They kill the overhead lights and Dana plugs in the black light, turning their toes into magic wands tipped with green flame. Dimension the likes of which oyster shell white could only dream of. Louise turns on some Europop and sets up the webcam so it captures only their feet from the ankles down as they dance. Louise with her prosthesis, Dana on her crutches.

"Okay." Louise gasps and hiccups her way back to the computer. "Let's post these little piggies."

"No!" Dana lurches toward the desk.

"Serious?" Louise's mouse hovers over the upload button. "You've let every Uber in town drive through your ass."

"Not on the internet."

Louise huffs. "Dana, this video is hot. You will be bringing untold joy to half a million freaks. Your feet will be legendary."

Dana unplugs the black light and rubs one bare foot on top of the other. "I remain anonymous? Promise?"

"Cross my heart," Louise says and clicks.

Dana reaches once more into her bag for a paper sack containing a marble mortar and pestle. "Can I leave this here for Francis?"

"Yeah, sure," Louise mumbles, already lost in her online world, typing furiously in the comments section.

Dana places a bow on the end of the pestle, leaves the set on Porky's workbench, and hikes upstairs, leaving Louise to her adoring fans. She finds Ben in the kitchen, opening then closing the microwave, before turning it on and standing to the side.

"So," he says. "You conjure the dark lord?"

"No, but I think my feet are porn stars." She notices the orange RAD indicator stickers on the microwave, the windows, the television, the stove. "What's going on?"

Ben stops the microwave and peers at the sticker. "Derm says the lesion on my arm isn't a fungal infection but it might be a burn. We're at risk of low-level radiation poisoning."

"From the dishwasher?"

"I read a thing in *Scientific American*. This microwave has gotta go." He absentmindedly palms his crotch. "I should get my sperm count checked."

She snorts. "Not like you're doing anything with them."

"Never say never, PharmD." He gives her a once-over. "Nice cardigan."

She glances down at her pilled, minivan-mom sweater. "Ben, as a scientific Canadian I can tell you that you're twenty-six years old, and unless you've been summering in Pripyat, your sperm are legion and rambunctious as they'll ever be. What's wrong with my cardigan?"

"I like your lab coat better."

"You would." She takes a page out of Louise's playbook and moves close enough that either of them could reach out and touch the other. "Can we talk? Maybe in the living room, away from all these radiators?"

"We're closer to the door here," he says, even as he halves the distance between them. "For when you run out on me."

"Don't be ridiculous."

Ben steps back and throws his arms out wide. "I am ridiculous, Dana. Slapping stickers all over the place. You think I don't know?"

"Then why do it?"

He pastes another on the Vitamix. "Because it's something I can do."

Dana snatches the stickers out of his hand and tosses them in the sink. "Get your coat. We're going for a walk."

"How far?"

"To the mall. Can you manage it?"

He swipes his salbutamol inhaler off the kitchen table. "Can you?"

His footsteps and her crutch-falls pop through the shopping complex, nearly deserted but for a few clusters of giggling stoners, also shambling in the general direction of the food court like a zombie herd. Ben tilts his face up to the pyramid skylight. "Saw a documentary on mall collapses. These skylights are points of structural weakness."

46

"Good, maybe the roof will fall and kill us instantly," Dana huffs, sounding breathless as Ben.

"Do you know the Shoppers Drug Mart guy?"

"On second thought," she says as they pass a dry reflecting pool littered with corroded pennies. "You'd be pinned under a beam until a feral cat ate your face."

Ben half smiles. "I knew it."

She halts, brandishing a crutch at him. "So what? Now you can call me a slut and feel better about how messed up you are?"

"Pump the brakes." He gently presses her crutch back to the ground. "I never called you a slut. And even if I did, it's not a value judgement."

"Then why would you ask about Callum?"

Ben shrugs. "Isn't that why we're here?"

Of course he would consider a trip to the pharmacy a form of recreation. Her aching hands relax around the padded aluminum handles. Her armpits are chafed and her trapezius muscles sing. She's put in a lot of crutch time today. Too much. "Let's get something to eat."

The patriarch's daughter is on duty at Wok-Wok. Dana remembers her name is Kiswar. And Kiswar remembers too, grinning slyly between Dana and Ben as she shovels greasy starch into Styrofoam. Once seated in the orange chairs, with their food set between them on the sticky table, Dana takes a moment to ground herself in that familiarity.

"I never met my father, but my mom always insisted she loved him," she says, knotting a noodle around her chopsticks. "When I was a kid I believed her."

"And now?" Ben asks.

"She loved falling in love. A lot. I doubt she knew for certain who my father was."

"A romantic."

"To the extreme. On both sides. Every time she broke up with a boyfriend I got my own personal performance of *La Traviata*."

Ben chases a shrimp around his bowl. "Turned you off the whole love thing pretty good."

"To say the least."

"But not sex."

"Obviously."

Ben pauses his half-hearted pursuit. "Why're you telling me this?"

"How else are we going to get to know each other?" She reaches into her bag and pulls out a bottle of Adderall capsules. "Here."

Ben's clammy fingers graze hers as she drops the rattling bottle into his hand. "Serious?"

"As a radioactive blender."

"Thought I was cut off."

"I never said that. But it's not free. You can pay next time you come in."

"Is this to keep me from going to your Shoppers guy?"

"Callum isn't my guy, and he's not interested in your satisfaction. Not like I am."

"But the legal stuff?"

Dana slurps up a noodle. "All I've done is fill a legit script as indicated for a diagnosed condition. On the record, I would advise that there are many alternative medications for ADHD. Off the record, I suspect the pronounced side effects of Adderall are more of a feature than a bug in your case."

Ben shoves the pills into his pocket and hunches into the crumpled question mark she knows so well. It's her turn for candour.

"I want to see where this goes, Ben. I just...don't exactly know where to go from here."

Ben bites off half a spring roll and offers up the remainder. "Here feels pretty good."

Dana resists clutching the door handle as Ben turns the steering wheel into their skid across the icy parking lot—full on a Sunday morning—and they nearly sideswipe a minivan before sliding into a vacant stall.

He cuts the ignition. "What?"

She lets out a tense breath. "You're a menace."

"You asked me to drive. And I got us here in one piece, didn't I?"

Dana grudgingly nods. Pity, as a collision would be an excuse to abort this outing entirely. Ben retrieves her crutches from the back seat, and helps get her situated, his hands chilling her through the thin fabric of her dress. She feels ridiculous not wearing a jacket, but the smallest things, like zippers, and feeding her arms in and out of sleeves, become an intolerable hassle with crutches. Together they shuffle their way across the ice toward the organ music grinding through the front door of Northside United Church.

"Smells like mouldy carpet," Ben says as they enter the warm chapel. "This place is probably insulated with asbestos."

"Stop it," Dana whispers. "If this...if 'us' is a thing now—"

"I'm a thing?"

"Then you have to do uncomfortable stuff with me."

"When you say uncomfortable, I imagine something different." He looks her over. "Especially in that dress."

Dana glances down at the only dress she owns. Dark blue, cocktail length, somewhat plunging neckline. She wears it to parties, weddings, and wakes. But never church. Until now.

"It's an hour of your life and it means a lot to Gwen and Marge."

"Don't forget *Rooolaaand*," he runs the name out as far as it will go and snaps it back on the last consonant.

Marge waves them over to the alcove leading to the restrooms, where she and Gwen are gathered with an elderly Filipino woman and a tall, slender man in Sunday-casual shirt and tie. Ben is dressed up in one of his nicer t-shirts, and a horrible sport coat. With his combed hair and smooth face, he looks like an infant.

Dana smiles and waves back before turning to Ben. "Why did you shave?"

"It's church," Ben says as they make their approach.

"Dana." Marge slips her arm around Dana's waist, grinning. "This is Iris and her boy, Roland."

"Pleasure," Dana replies. And it is. Some people radiate goodness, and Roland, with his relaxed posture and kind smile, is one of them. She returns the smile, then nods toward her twitchy companion.

"And this is Ben."

Roland's thoughtful eyes linger on hers before he turns, extending his hand to Ben. "Good to meet you."

Ben clears his throat. "Heya. Um, it's kind of a weird thing but I don't shake."

Iris nods. "Filthy custom."

"Right?" Ben says.

"You're a smart boy." Iris pats Ben's forearm. "I'll bet you're on the honour roll."

Roland catches Dana's eye and another smile wings across his face. "Nice to meet you both. Mom, we should grab a seat. Dana, do you need a hand?"

"I can manage for now," Dana says, her hunch about Roland's goodness confirmed. "But thank you for offering."

"They're about to start, Margie," Gwen interjects. "Swell to see you, Dana, and with a fella no less."

Dana flushes.

"Wow," Ben says as they slide into a pew near the back.

"You couldn't just shake his hand?" Dana sets her crutches aside, gracelessly dropping her backside down on thinly cushioned wood.

"Didn't Marge say he was ugly?" asks Ben.

"Feeling threatened?"

"Why?" He looks at her like she's the biggest airhead alive.

"Because three old ladies set my girlfriend up with a tall, handsome guy?"

"Ben," Dana says, her systolic pressure spiking.

"And I'm in church for some fucking reason. Why would I feel threatened?"

She presses her fingertips to her drumming temples. "You know, forget it, let's just survive this."

Organ music resumes and the congregation sings the opening hymn. Dana barely hears them. Girlfriend? He of all people should understand what a loaded word that is. And the first time he says it is in the context of a mean-spirited joke? Anger is the right reaction here. So why does she want to cry?

The hymn ends and rolls immediately into the invocation prayer.

50

Dana keeps her hands clasped in her lap. Ben fidgets, hands tapping his legs, sliding in and out of his jacket pockets, winding in and out of fists. Sitting still for an hour is no easy thing. At least Roland and his elderly companions are three rows ahead. Dana watches his head dip as Iris speaks to him. He listens and nods. Then he glances over his shoulder and catches Dana's eye with another of his easy smiles.

Ben whispers, "You got a rubber in your purse?"

"What?"

"You heard me."

She hesitates. "Well...yes."

"Then I dare you to take Roland into the bathroom and give him a religious experience."

Her stomach clenches. "You can't be serious."

"Why not? We're here. He's sitting in front of us and still can't keep his eyes off your tits. Story writes itself."

"You've read too many *Penthouse Letters*."

Ben gives her a blank look.

"Jesus." Dana buries her face in her hand. "You're just a baby."

A trio of blue-hairs turn to glare at them. Ben leans forward. "Baby Jesus, she digs him."

Two of the ladies pucker into further disapproval, but the last winks at Dana before facing around.

Ben grins. "Golden girl number three says go for it."

"We're in a church."

"A United Church."

"You're messing with me because I made you come here?"

"You don't have to," he says. "Just thought if that stick has a chance, so does Roland."

"Stick?"

"The one up your ass, PharmD."

For a voluntarily celibate person, Ben has a filthy imagination. He's getting off on this idea. Any resistance melts away in the heat of increasing restlessness. She's been off HOok for weeks.

The minister gives an animated sermon of Jesus walking on water, the lesson being that faith is powerful but common sense is its own everyday miracle.

"One of God's most underrated gifts," the minister declares, her dimpled smile visible all the way to the back row. "May not grab the biblical spotlight, may not be sexy, may not let us walk on water, but it will keep us from drowning ourselves. So, listen to that still-small voice, and let us pray."

"Common sense isn't sexy," says Ben. "If that's not a sign from God..."

"The still-small voice says this is a bad idea."

Ben's hand creeps onto her thigh and slides down until his fingers dip under the rigid edge of her knee brace and it is unspeakably intimate.

"We're both going to hell," Dana murmurs, though she can't deny the dilating blood vessels under her skin. "You need to distract Mother while I bag Norman."

"Gotcha."

They bump fists as a sea of amens washes over the congregation, and the organ winds up, ending the service. Ben scuttles through the crowd, cutting Iris away. Dana finds Roland in the front of the church, one shoulder leaning against a pillar. Self-assured, relaxed, and so utterly normal it's almost off-putting. She watches him observe Ben in conversation with Iris.

Dana sidles up on her crutches. "This is weird, huh?"

Roland nods. "Their plan was weird. The execution is somehow more tragic."

Dana cuts right to the chase. "Roland, I'm going to visit the accessible restroom for a few minutes. Would you like to join me?"

Roland clearly does not understand. And then he does. "Uh, what about...?"

"The boy?" Dana asks over her shoulder, already hopping away. "What about him?"

She plans to picture Ben, imagine it's his body colliding with hers, but Roland makes that impossible. Roland is Roland. Gentle and fumbling. Lacking anything like Ben's deliberate slowness. Which she can't fault him for because this whole scenario is a fever dream set to dissolve at any moment. Nevertheless, they are two

52

adults more or less competent at sex. He checks in, early and often. Asking if it's good, if her leg is okay. She drags his hand to where it's more than just okay. Roland is not Ben. It takes longer than is ideal. Orgasm can be elusive in the house of God.

They emerge from the bathroom together and join the others in the foyer. She expects some kind of nod from Ben but he won't look at her, not even in the sideways manner he prefers when eye contact is not an option.

"Where've you two been?" Iris asks Roland. "Abandoning this nervous boy with a bunch of old ladies."

"My fault." Dana makes a show of leaning on her crutches. "I somehow locked myself in the accessible restroom. Roland happened to hear me banging away and came to my rescue."

"I raised a gentleman," Iris says, beaming. "My sugars are feeling low, Rollie. Shall we go for lunch?"

"Let's," Marge says and turns to Dana. "You and Ben will come, won't you?"

Ben hunches into his jacket and takes a step back.

"Thanks, Marge," Dana replies. "But I need to put my leg up. Iris, Roland, it was lovely to meet you." Iris insists on a hug, and Dana takes the opportunity to hug Roland too. Mostly to spite Ben, though surprisingly, the rush of loathing she expects with the embrace never arrives.

"Nice to meet you, Ben," Iris pats his arm once more. "You're a good boy, taking your mum to church. I hope we see you again."

You will NEVER see me again, thinks Dana as she and Ben make their awkward exit.

Ben slides into the driver's side once more because Dana's knee really is killing her after seven minutes in heaven.

"What the hell was that all about?" Ben says, as he swerves into traffic.

"Me looking old enough to have a twenty-six-year-old son?"

"I mean slobbering over Roland."

"Need I remind you this was your idea?"

"You didn't have to do it."

"So, it was a test?" Dana twists in her seat. "A trap? You can't fuck me so you fuck with me, instead?"

"No. I just..." He tightens his grip on the wheel. "You walked out of there looking happy and satisfied. You gave Roland the Sunday Service of a lifetime, and I'm an asshole because I can't...let you have that."

Dana squeezes her eyes shut. "I really don't understand what's happening right now."

Ben drives in silence, down slick streets lined with hoar-frosted poplars.

"You know I want it to be you," she says.

He ignores her so perfectly, she questions whether she said the words out loud.

She tries again. "Maybe one day?"

The world spins for a moment when Ben wrenches the wheel and they pull into a driveway and Dana realizes they aren't at his place, but hers. "How do you know where I live?"

"Lou got it when she booked your ride that night."

Ben comes around to the passenger side to help her out. She's still in his arms, settling onto her crutches, when she asks, "Do you want to come in?"

"Maybe another time."

She drops her head to her chest, refusing to let him see how much he's hurt her. "How are you getting home?"

"I'll catch the bus." He releases her and strolls down her driveway. "See ya, PharmD."

She's angry. All afternoon she's angry. Enough to clumsily vacuum and scrub her shower tiles, in the middle of which she circles back to the realization that she's completely bypassed the usual skin-crawling disgust following a sexual encounter. Distraction? She's furious at Ben—petulant child—so that's likely. As a test she imagines Roland's breath on her neck, his hands on her skin. Her ears start to ring and her stomach roils with familiar enteric disturbance. She wriggles out of her clothes and cranks the shower on as hot as she can stand. She's not cured, and it's too marginal and isolated to be conclusive progress.

But it isn't nothing.

54

She's reaching for her crutches to hoist herself out of the bathtub when the phone rings.

"Hello?"

"Is Benny with you?" asks Louise. "He's not answering his phone. Figured you two might be doing it."

Dana wraps herself in a towel. "He dropped me off hours ago. Said he'd catch the bus home."

"Then why isn't he answering?"

"Ben is a grown-up, Louise. I wouldn't worry about him."

"Don't patronize me, slut. I'm not his keeper, but he always checks in and he's usually home by now to take his meds. You sure he said he was catching the bus?"

"You think I'm lying?"

"*Are* you?"

"Goodbye, Louise."

Dana dries her hair and looks in the mirror. On paper, she resembles her mother: same hazel eyes, and triangular fox-like features, only Dana's are smaller, less generous. Impish. Her mother always called her that, *imp*, but rounded it off with so much love, the final "p" lacked any judgemental clout. She pulls her hair back; it's a little better. This time she struggles into a jacket before grabbing her purse, and heading out the door again.

The barber shop is open and has a picture of a man in the window with more or less the long, asymmetric pixie cut she has in mind. Pasha, the proprietor, is at first taken aback by a woman on crutches struggling through the door of his shop, but then throws himself into his work with enthusiasm, singing in Russian as he snips, and she observes her appropriate locks fall on the front of her smock like golden fleece. Finally, after some product and an artful blowout, Pasha declares her to be a blonde Lily Collins, whoever that is.

Settled once again in the car, Dana checks her slightly wild new look in the rearview and is about to google Lily Collins when something buzzes on the floor. It's Ben's phone.

"Louise?"

"Slut?"

"I'd like it if you didn't call me that."

"Put Benny on."

"He's not here, he left his phone in my car."

"Fuck, we gotta find him."

"I'm sure he's fine."

"You don't understand. He needs his treatment. If he gets an infection... If his lungs act up he's got no way to call for help."

Unease prickles her freshly exposed nape. "I'm going to drive around and have a look, okay?"

She drives slowly, like someone on the lookout for their runaway dog, down the most likely walking route and then doubles back to take the less likely routes. No sign of Ben. She's about to drive to the mall when her phone rings. Blood crystalizes in every capillary. It's the police.

Dana's crutch slips on a patch of ice as she hikes too fast across the tiny parking lot and stumbles into the lobby of the downtown city jail and remand centre. The officer at the desk goes into the back to make a call. Shortly thereafter, another officer comes through the doors into the waiting area. Her name, pinned to her stout chest, reads Const. T. Partridge.

"Fuck," Dana mutters before she can think better of it.

Partridge either doesn't hear or doesn't react. "Ma'am, would you mind coming around back?"

Dana follows her to a tidy desk so small that Ms. Partridge, now Constable T., seems to wear it like a belt rather than use it as a work surface. "Ms... Can I call you Dana?"

"Can I call you T?" Dana doesn't know where the glib retort comes from.

"Stands for Theodora, but you know that."

Dana clamps her mouth shut, not trusting what might fly out next. Ben is guilty of a number of crimes she knows about and likely a lot more she doesn't. The less she says, the better.

"Call me Ted, everyone does," she says, unsmiling but with a softening in her eyes.

"Okay...Ted. I'm confused about what's happening. The officer on the phone mentioned social disorder?"

"Which means this isn't a criminal matter."

"Then why is he here? Something must have happened. What did he do?"

Ted leans back in her chair, relaxed, or pretending to be. "It's nothing serious."

"Social disorder doesn't sound like nothing serious."

"It's just a term."

Dana fights to keep her voice modulated. "For what?"

"For being a nuisance, basically."

She inhales through her nose and holds it. Come on, *vagus nerve*. "Dana."

"Ted."

A quirk of a smile as Ted splays her heavy hands on her tiny desk. "Is he hurt?" Dana prods.

"He's safe." Ted drums her fingers on the oak veneer "Can I ask why he'd have us call you?"

"I guess...because I could come get him."

"Is that your relationship?"

Dana couldn't answer that if she wanted to.

Ted leans in. "We're concerned about Mr. Kidd's welfare. Does he have a history of mental illness, problems with drugs or alcohol?"

Is Ted asking her as Ben's friend, or as his pharmacist? Dana's stomach gurgles. She hasn't eaten a thing all day. She thinks she might vomit into Ted's wastebasket full of crumpled sticky notes.

"Benjamin Kidd does not have a criminal record, though he is known to police," Ted says with an almost amused look. "That's not why we picked him up today."

"Can you please tell me what happened?" Dana whispers. "I need to see him. I just need to know he's all right."

Ted lays a hand over Dana's clenched fists. Her touch is warm and shockingly gentle considering the eagle wing span of those fingers. "Easy, okay? I'm here to help."

Ten minutes later Dana is back in the waiting room, wrenching herself out of a plastic chair as Ben scurries through a set of double doors.

His eyes widen. "Wow, your hair."

"I've spent the last two hours looking everywhere for you."

"Thanks for bailing me out."

"I didn't bail you out. You weren't in jail; you're not charged with anything." She slaps his phone into his chest. "Call Louise, she's worried."

Ben dials, and as he speaks to Louise, Dana notices his hands are bright pink, his face grey, and his halting sentences not a product of Louise interrupting, but shortness of breath.

"I'm fine...yeah, I-I'm fine...huh..." His eyes become glassy, his lips tinged blue around the edges.

Dana grabs the phone from him. "Louise?"

"Dana."

"We're on our way," she says, hanging up and using her crutch to push the automatic door button.

Ben coughs wetly into his sleeve as they make their way to the car. "I didn't plan on getting arrested for jaywalking. And I'm sure as hell not drunk. Why're you and Lou so ornery?"

"Because we love you, idiot. Now get in," Dana snaps, collapsing into the driver's side.

Ben buckles his seatbelt. He reaches over and threads his fingers through the longer layers of her shorn hair. "Off kilter. I like it."

Her heart squeezes. On rare occasions, Dana's mom would look at her a certain way, focusing all her love on her daughter rather than splitting it with the boyfriend of the season. Ben looks at her that way now. Undivided. Like she's his world.

"Ben, are you all right? Constable Partridge told me what happened."

"Yeah, she got twitchy, cuz I didn't have ID and wouldn't tell her my name."

"She said you were behaving strangely."

"Carding is a fascist method of social control."

"Oh for Christ's sake." Dana slaps her palm on the dash. "This isn't the man trying to keep you down. She said she was concerned you would come to harm."

Ben drops his head back and closes his eyes. "After I left your place, I didn't catch the bus, I just wandered. I dunno, I was like, locked in my head. Crossed the street, and nearly got smeared by a car, happens to be a cruiser. At that point I'm so tied up in knots I can hardly think let alone talk. No wonder she thought I was belligerent."

Dana doesn't argue, but Ted Partridge had her heart in the right place. She could have been petty and made things a lot more difficult, instead she'd thanked Dana for coming and seemed grateful that Ben had a safe place to go and people to look after him. Ted sincerely cared.

Ben doesn't speak the rest of the way to his house, just coughing into his elbow and wheezing. Dana insists on coming inside.

"I'm fine," he protests.

"You're shivering. You were out in the cold for hours without anything but this horrible jacket. Probably hypothermic."

They trip into the house as thick coughs wrack Ben's body. He twists away when she lays a hand on his back.

"Don't," he rasps.

"Ben, you're sick."

"Back off," he snarls, and lurches down the hall, the bathroom door slamming behind him, followed by the hiss of water that doesn't quite cover up the sound of coughing or vomiting or both.

Louise steps into the foyer. "Thanks for bringing him home."

"Should I take him to the hospital? He's in respiratory distress."

"Naw, we got this."

Porky emerges from the living room, with the barest nod for Dana.

"Grab his meds and get him into a hot bath," Louise says. "I'll get his vest out of the closet."

Porky hesitates. "He won't like being disturbed."

"I don't give a fuck what he likes. Either you do it, or I will."

Porky trundles down the hall and Dana wonders about the

vest. Does Louise mean the life jacket? Is Ben that likely to drown in the bathtub? She's about to ask when Louise hands Dana her crutches. "Don't worry, sis. We'll take care of him."

"Maybe I should stay, in case he needs anything."

"He needs you not to see him like this." Louise continues hustling her out the door. "Love the hair, by the way. You look like Lily Collins."

Monday passes in unending tedium as Dana stays home and attempts to let her swollen knee recover from the previous day's drama. At some point she concludes that the condo she's lived in for over five years could easily pass for a residential hotel, tastefully appointed but utterly devoid of personality. She lives there, but it's not a home. Not like the pharmacy. And not like Ben's house.

Tuesday morning finally arrives with fluffy white flakes the size of hummingbirds. Dana goes in early to do her weekly batch compounding. Winter months see an increase in demand for just about everything from antibiotics to anti-depressants. She blends up a batch of liquid amoxicillin for the inevitable ear infections and bronchitis that developed over the weekend. She stores the jars of banana- and strawberry-flavoured syrup in the fridge. Topical steroid stores are running low as well. She piles hydrocortisone powder onto a marble slate, using a spatula to combine it with a mineral oil ointment. Eczema is another condition exacerbated by the cold, dry weather, and Dana recommends the ointment over the less efficacious cream.

Wintry air wafts through the dispensary as the back door opens and closes.

"Good morning, Marge."

"You too, chickie—Oh!"

Dana glances up through the bangs slanting over her forehead. "Lily Collins?"

"Who?"

"Right?" Dana holds up her purple nitrile hands.

Marge places a palm over her heart. "You look darling. Really."

"But?"

"Like one of them pretty homosexuals on the nighttime soaps." Marge stows her purse in the locking cupboard and takes the kettle to the sink. "Now, I'm going to make us a cup of tea and you're going to tell Margie what you did or what you're about to do."

Dana shakes her head. "Why?"

Marge pauses. "Why not?"

"Because it's weird that my best friend is an old lady in my employ."

"Are you firing me?"

"Never," Dana says, sitting up straight as a javelin. "Nor are you permitted to quit or die."

Marge plugs in the kettle and scrutinizes her. "Honey, did something happen at church?"

"Other than me bringing my adult son, just like Iris?"

Marge giggles. "Iris was taken with him."

"Don't suppose anyone bothered to tell her."

"Oh, she knew." Marge waves it off with another witchy laugh. "What's the point being old if you can't mess with the young'uns. Iris admires your moxie, having such a young beau, even if it meant her boy struck out."

Dana clenches her jaw. Roland is a lovely man. And she'd rather chew aluminum foil than let him touch her again. Probably.

"So, you and Ben are an item?"

"I don't know, truly."

"I gotcha." Marge pulls on her smock and drops teabags in a couple of mugs. "Folks these days want to knock boots without putting a label on it; that's their business."

"We haven't. Boots on or off." Dana scrapes the prepared cortisone ointment into a pot.

The kettle whistles and Marge fills the mugs. "Taking it slow?"

"Standing still. We hang out with his housemates, take care of his plants, loiter at the mall, cook together, argue about radiation poisoning—I brought him to church, for Christ's sake. I even bailed him out of jail. We do everything couples do—except what couples do."

"Jail?" Marge looks up so fast her glasses slip off her nose.

"Jaywalking." Dana reminds herself that Ben is, in fact, a criminal and could one day be properly arrested. "Got a bit out of hand."

"No one is perfect." Marge hands her a cup of Earl Grey.

They move to the tiny table in the break area, sitting side by side, and blowing on their hot tea.

"Ben collects freaks," Dana says. "I'm just his latest acquisition."

"Honey, that little weirdo is in love with you. Plain as red paint on a white wall." Marge sips her tea, leaving cakey pink lipstick on the rim. "Look, the world's full of regular folks and I'm not ashamed to admit I'm one of them. It's odd ducks like you, Ben, and tricksy old Iris that save the world from death by beige."

Dana ponders this. "Oyster shell has hidden dimensions."

Marge flicks her fingers through Dana's hair. "Methinks you're done hiding."

Louise answers the door, snapping her gum as usual. "Hey, sis. Leave your shoes on."

Dana knows better than to ask for an explanation, crutching her way down the hall after Louise, where Porky sidles by without so much as looking at her.

"Is he feeling better?" Dana asks once they've made their way to the back door.

Louise pauses with her hand on the knob. "Still mad at him?"

"Don't I have a right to be?"

"Benny does a lot that's 'bad' by society's standards, and he fucks up plenty, but he's the best person I know."

Dana gauges the risk. This is her chance, but if she wants honesty from Louise, she won't get it without first offering in kind. "I care...a lot." Dana winces at her oyster shell of emotional honesty.

"What I mean is...he...I have feelings...it's..."

"Damn girl, don't give yourself a stroke," Louise says. "You're falling for him. And you're scared."

"Shitless."

"Much better." Louise grins. Her approval elicits a visceral warmth and Dana understands that Louise's friendship is no shallow thing. If one is lucky enough to have it, it's ride or die. But it must be earned.

"Louise, is there anything I should know about Ben? I mean, mentally?"

Louise drags her prosthetic foot up the inside of her thigh, standing in tree pose. "He'd never hurt you. Not on purpose. And as far as I know he's got no wish to hurt himself."

"That's a careful response."

"I meant what I said, he's the best person I know, but also he's a damn liar and a good one."

"What else has he lied to me about?"

Louise sways, one-legged, before wobbling and lowering her prosthetic. "Probably not much outright, but that's the trick of it. Using a sparkly piece of truth to steer you away from the bits that aren't so pretty. He's out back." She opens the door onto a tidy yard. "Good luck, sis."

Dana navigates frosty pavers to the large greenhouse next to the garage. The door swings awkwardly outward, and she curses as her crutch slips on the thin wash of ice. Warm air billows out and pulls her into the humid jungle. The planter in the living room consists mostly of ferns, palms, and succulents. The greenhouse appears to grow tomatoes, rosemary, sage, thyme, and marijuana. The cannabis isn't flowering, so the intermingled odours are only mildly herbal.

"Ben?"

"Stay there," he says from inside the greenery. "Don't move."

"Is this place booby-trapped?"

"Just easier to say this when I can't see you. Though, to be honest, I figured you'd save me the trouble."

Dana rubs a marijuana leaf between her fingers. He's going to dump her. Probably for the best. And it does save her the trouble.

"Yesterday was a clusterfuck."

Dana laughs. "Indisputably."

"Mostly my fault."

"I'd argue all your fault, but okay." She peers into the foliage, trying to catch a glimpse of him.

"Dragging a degenerate like me to church? That's on you."

Already she misses him. A novel experience in itself. "Seems you're feeling better."

"Enough to be deadly embarrassed." He pauses. "Dana, I want to promise you nothing like that'll happen again."

The words pierce her shroud of resignation. "Benjamin, I'm confused."

"So'm I—you sound exactly like my mother."

"Are you apologizing or breaking up with me?"

"Didn't you come here to break up with me?"

"I came to see if you were okay."

"Could've called," he says.

That is patently absurd. They've never spoken on the phone or even texted. All interactions are carried out in person. Lo-fi, lo-tech. She doubts they could communicate any other way. Which is also absurd.

He sighs. "You know I'm gonna mess up, right?"

"Seems likely we both will."

"And what about being normal? Seems to mean something to you."

His earnest tone softens her, and she plucks a wilted basil leaf, bringing it to her nose. It's safe here. Safe to tell the truth.

"It does, but I'm getting over it."

Silence, more rustling, and more silence. "Well...what now?"

Dana thinks about it. "Show me what you're doing back there?"

"Step into my jungle, PharmD."

Dana's heart canters as she gently bushwhacks her way to the rear of the greenhouse. Ben comes into view. A tousled gnome among giant blossoms of white, crimson, and pink. Four petals with a black heart.

"Afraid you've caught me with my other lady friends. There's

64

about a hundred, fortunately they're all named Poppy. Makes it easier. Girls, this is Dana."

Dana studies the exquisite blooms on some of the plants and the egg-sized seed pods on others. "Tell me this isn't what I think it is."

"Depends what you think."

"Why are you growing these?"

"Same reason I dig you. They're pretty and they smell good. Tasty too."

"You expect me to believe you grow opium poppies purely for their ability to transform a bagel?"

"Primarily, but waste not want not." Using a three-tined blade, he scores one of the plump green seed pods. Milky sap beads along the incisions.

"This is illegal," she says, hearing how mom-ish it sounds and feeling every year of their considerable age gap.

"This is hardly a crop, and it's not like I'm making heroin. You of all people ought to know p. somniferum has a long history of treating all kinds of conditions, from epilepsy, respiratory disorders, anxiety, pancreatic insufficiency."

"Sexual dysfunction."

Ben shoots her a look halfway between disdain and innuendo. "Hysteria."

"Bloodletting and dockside tooth extraction were also common in the olden days, before science and laws."

"Laws are for people who can't think."

"Thinking and addictive alkaloids historically haven't burned up the bedsheets together."

He points at her with the sticky blade. "In Asia, opium consumption is as casual as having a beer on a hot day. It's less addictive than alcohol. Put that in your pipe and smoke it, PharmD."

"You've been to Asia?"

"Born in Kolkata."

She squints. "Be gone."

"I know, right? Whitest Indian guy you'll ever meet. My mom is a Brit, a biologist. Dad was a poet. They met at the university. I was a sick kid from the get-go, so Mom got a job at UofT and off we went to Canada where they had better health care. Still spent a few months a year in Asia on research grants, stewing through some jungle or freezing on a highland plain."

"Your father *was* a poet?"

"Till the day he died. You'd think it would be some exotic parasite, or one of those duct-tape prop jobs we were always almost-crashing in, but nope. In the end it was the summer we stayed in Toronto, in 2003."

Ben's paranoia around disease suddenly makes sense.

"SARS," she says, moving closer and setting a light hand on his arm.

Ben nods. "I was five. Wish I remembered him better. Sometimes...I hear his voice, a word in Bengali here and there."

"And your mom?"

"Still splits her time between lab and land. We video chat now and then, usually at three in the morning."

"You're not close?"

"Mom plants poppies and counts the seconds until the petals fall off." He scores another pod, bleeding the milky fluid. "It's always about the end, or what's next. It's hard for her to be in the moment. She's great, though." He frowns slightly. "Moms can be that way. Messed up but still good, you know?"

Dana knows, and an acute longing knifes into her heart. *Listen here, imp. Too many people waste their life waiting to die.* Dana could argue that her mom did waste her life, on loving men who didn't love her back, but she certainly never waited for death. A massive stroke took her when Dana was in her final year at university. Gone before she hit her kitchen floor.

"I never got to say goodbye to my mom." Dana leans into a white bloom the size of her splayed hand and inhales the sundrenched perfume. Petals stroke her cheeks and Ben's fingertips are on her jaw, raising her face to his.

"Field hands would lick the knife between scorings, kept the blade from gumming up with sap and the workers compliant." He drags the dull edge of the lancet across her lips, leaving a smear of sticky latex behind. A challenge, a dare.

66

Instead of licking it off, she darts forward and kisses him.

Dana is the aggressor, tasting the bitter poppies, a dark mirror of their sunny scent. The earthy spice of oblivion. She's the aggressor—until her crutches are flung into the embrace of a large marijuana plant and she finds herself pinned to the warm greenhouse glass wall.

"Yesterday," Ben whispers, teeth scraping over her lip, hands sliding under her shirt. "Did Roland get you off?"

"He did his best. I did the heavy lifting."

Sweat pearls along her hairline as his fingers press hard between her ribs. She slides her arms around his bony shoulders. He groans as her hips lift, and his rough voice pours into her mouth. "I want that. I want to make you come, Dana."

If words alone could make it happen, it would be happening now. Then Ben's chest gives a rattling hitch, bringing her back to all the reasons this is a bad idea. She pushes his hands out of her shirt. "Ben."

He backs off, breathing with deep intent. Then he looks right into her eyes, something still so rare it mesmerizes her. Her head feels loose, as though it might tumble off her shoulders and crack on the concrete like a pumpkin.

"What are you doing to me?" she chokes.

The look on his face breaks her heart. The battery scam, the amphetamines, the weeping poppy pods, he could have easily kept it all secret. They're a test. Barriers he's throwing in her path.

"You ought to run," he says.

"How?" She snags her crutches out of the foliage. "You've literally hobbled me."

"That's the last thing I want." He takes her face between his hands, but gently. "Yesterday in church, I was trying to show you."

"Show me what?"

"That I don't expect you to change the way you live out there."

She turns her head and kisses his palm, stained with hot-house green. "Right now, I'm here."

This is their covenant, and it feels strangely biblical.

Yesterday, under God's very roof, Ben tempted her into sin, and today he plies her with the blood of poppies. Angelic and insidious.

Each time she's on the cusp of escape, the Devil lures her back with something tantalizing.

It's another snowy evening just before close when the door chimes in the front. Dana is locking up cabinets and decides if they need something mixed up it'll have to wait until tomorrow.

"What happened to you?"

The voice asking the endlessly repeated question is gruff. Dana turns to face Callum standing on the other side of the counter. She touches her hair. "Needed a change, I guess."

He points a finger. "I meant the cane."

"Recent upgrade from crutches." Dana's voice wavers and she clears her throat. She's nervous. Extremely nervous. But the bolt of revulsion she's braced for doesn't strike.

"How'd you manage that?" he asks.

"Awkward social exit. What are you doing here?"

"I was in the neighbourhood."

"Uh huh." Dana lets the silence stretch, buying her time to slip into more confident emotional armour.

Callum pushes his finger and thumb under the bridge of his glasses to rub his nose. "Am I that transparent?"

"Wandering in ten minutes before close? I invented that move."

"In my defence I'm recently divorced. Terribly out of practice."

"Not that terrible," she says, fingertips moving across the counter in a sensual glide. Is she actually flirting?

He smiles, and she's reminded of a children's craft set where you mix and match facial features, creating ghoulish approximations of human expression.

"Thought maybe we could grab that beer," he says.

"I'd like that." And she really would, because she really does like Callum. She'd like to see how long this newfound tolerance for a former lover's presence will last. With Roland it was a few hours. Perhaps with repeat exposure she'll become desensitized and, dare she even think it, cured? "Another time? I've got plans."

Callum leans in. "Look, this isn't a purely social call. Someone came in today, asking about Benjamin Kidd. A Constable Partridge?"

Dana inhales slowly.

"I didn't give her any specifics, only that he'd taken his business to another shop. Probably since mine is closing."

"Is that true?"

"Been on the chopping block for years." He shrugs. "Place is a deadzone, you may have noticed. Come spring, I'm transferring downtown. Anyway, Partridge didn't seem to think anything of it until I mentioned it was your shop he went to."

"Is she investigating Ben?"

Callum rocks his head side to side. "Felt off the books. She wasn't on duty, but she did ask what kinds of compounding you do."

"Why?"

"I don't know. But I do know cops don't go after the Bens of the world. Not when they can go after bigger fish. Like their suppliers."

Dana clenches her back molars against a sudden wave of nausea. "You think I'm filling bogus scripts?"

"I think you should stay out of trouble." Callum raps his knuckles on the counter. "Because I'd really like to grab that beer sometime."

Marge moseys over after Callum leaves. "Do you actually have plans tonight?"

"No." Dana reaches under the counter and retrieves the wastebasket.

"That rugged grump is sweet on you."

"He's the pharmacist at the Spruce Cliff Shoppers, and I already slept with him," she blurts, and with a brutal heave, vomits into the trash.

"Oh, chickie. You're not pregnant, are you?"

"Jesus, Marge," she gasps, scraping her sweaty hair off her forehead.

"Calls 'em like I sees 'em. Between twenty-something boy toys, lumberjack chemists, and canoodling in church toilets."

"Did Roland tell you?"

"I'm not blind, chickie. Know well enough the look of a man that's just had his pin pulled. All these years Gwen and I wondered if you were a robot with her knees welded together. Turns out you got a juicier love life than most."

"I'm not pregnant. And don't say juicy."

"Glamourous then. Like a soap opera."

Truly, it's orders of magnitude less glamorous than that. Sex, drugs, fraud, broken bones, bad lungs, and a house full of misfits she desperately wants to win over, if only she could stop stepping in it every time she darkens their door. Now the police are involved, if only in the form of off-duty Constable Ted Partridge. This is not good. It's not smart. It's not romantic. And it won't end well. She needs to put some space between her damage and Ben's.

Marge returns with a bottle of water and a pregnancy test. "Set an old lady's mind at ease?"

An hour later, with a promise to inform Marge of the results, Dana is at home, on the toilet, peeing on a stick. And a little over her hand. While her stomach continues to churn.

She sets the test on the vanity and wanders into her generic kitchen, taking a seat on one of the modern Danish bar stools. Her phone dings and she pulls it from her pocket, nearly dropping it on the tile floor. *We miss you! Drop us a line!* A notification from HOok, even though she muted her account weeks ago.

She'll delete it.

Tomorrow. Probably.

Three minutes to go.

Between an IUD, insistence on condoms, and her age, pregnancy is unlikely. She's never yearned for children and always knew what she'd do if she ever found herself pregnant. That hasn't changed.

70

But the reality that she'll have to go through it by herself stings like never before. She's alone. Of course there's Marge, but Dana is her employer and that says something. Ben was right about that.

Dana would go to the clinic alone, have the procedure alone, with only Katie in her Acura to drive her home.

Two minutes.

Of course, it's early enough that a dose of mifepristone will destabilize any zygote nesting in her reproductive organs. But there's no one to hold her hand when she starts to cramp and bleed. Even Constable Partridge has someone to rub diclofenac into her lumbar spine, Dana can tell. Partridge is cared for, the way someone who is not can spot immediately. Someone who has no one to ice their broken patella, for example.

One minute.

Dana's stomach rolls again, and has her thinking about Ben's poppies. About narcotics and their accompanying nausea. Theoretically, one could create an emulsion of opium and cannabis oil. To be taken orally or even vaporized. Add a little lavender for the smell, or sandalwood; she could ask Porky...

The timer dings and Dana hustles into the bathroom to check.

Not pregnant.

Before she has time to let her doubts gather, she texts Marge a photo of the negative test, grabs her keys and her cane, and heads out the door.

The culture of a relationship is defined by its routines as much as the personalities of those involved. Dana isn't sure when she became the type of person to drop in on people unannounced, but the pattern comforts her. The habit is unconscious, even as she turns in the direction of Ben's house, even recalling her vow to keep her distance. As long as she's not unwelcome, she can't seem to stay away.

Ben answers the door, lounging against the frame in a band

shirt faded to illegibility.

"I brought something." She holds up a branded RESPIRO duffel bag. "Like a game. One I thought maybe...maybe we could all play?"

"Team building?" he asks. "You already won Louise over with the foot party."

Dana stares at her salt-crusted boots. "But not Porky."

"He'll get there."

In the living room, Ben opens the basement door and yells down, "Hey, we got company."

Commotion and hissed whispering follow, then galumphing up the stairs, and Louise emerges, wide-eyed, with a similarly panicked Porky behind her. Her eyes land on Dana and she glares at Ben. "We thought you meant the cops, you shit."

Ben shoots her an annoyed look. "We got a safe word for that."

"Blueberry," Porky says to Dana, his expression flat and unreadable once more as he adjusts the bulky hearing aid curving around one ear.

"I brought something." Dana pulls the white plastic module out of the bag. "Developed by a local respiratory homecare company, and I'm thinking of setting it up at the store. Self-administered pulmonary function tests. Like the blood pressure machines." She caps a disposable sleeve over the mouthpiece and plugs the cord into her phone. "An app takes the readings and plots your volume and flow on a graph. I was hoping you all might help me figure out how buggy it is."

"Ben, you want to go first?" Dana asks, surprised when he shakes his head. "Why not?"

"Don't need that to show me my lungs are a disaster."

"I'll try," says Porky.

Dana reads off the prompts: inhale, hold, hard exhale. Three times to get accurate results. "Francis, your lung function is excellent according to the app."

"Do me." Louise snags the module from Porky's hand and stuffs it in her mouth without changing the sleeve. Louise's results are also healthy and consistent, which means the equipment is fairly user friendly. Dana tries as well.

72

"Okay, so we have a baseline," she says. "But I wonder if we ought to experiment further. In the name of science."

"Science?" Ben's lips quirk up in a little smile. "What did you have in mind?"

"I'm interested in the short-term effects of smoking marijuana on pulmonary function."

"You serious?"

"Where's your stash?"

Ben squeezes her arm and heads down to the basement. Louise gives her a strange look. Porky stares intently at Louise.

"What?" Dana says. "It's market research. I've had inquiries about partnering with dispensaries to develop cannabis-infused products."

"You smoke pot?" Louise asks.

Dana clears her throat. "Never, actually. But I'm willing to try."

"For science?"

Dana nods as Ben emerges from the basement with a polished wood box. He opens it, and within minutes, rolls a perfect joint.

"I, um, thought we might vape it," Dana says.

Ben shakes his head. "Nope, we're bootin' it old style tonight."

"I'm not sure..." She hesitates, her palms growing damp.

"You're a virgin, I get it." Ben licks the rolling paper and winks. "I'll make it good for you, PharmD."

He lights the joint with a match, takes a shallow pull, and passes it to Louise who takes a veteran drag. Porky does the same, and when the slim cigarette makes its way to Dana, Ben swipes it out of her fingers. "Let me." He takes a long, deep pull.

"Ben, your asthma."

He wraps his hand around the back of her neck. She thinks he's going to kiss her, but instead he blows a slender tube of musty-sweet smoke into her mouth, and in her surprise, she inhales with perfect synchronicity.

"Less harsh this way," Ben says, his voice sandpaper rough. "Keep it in for a sec."

Dana lets the urge to cough bang around in her throat. Ben's smoky breath curls in her lungs, conforming to the shape of her anatomy. Then she exhales gracelessly into his face.

"Nicely done," he laughs.

And there it is again, that look of total acceptance. Only now does she realize how much she's missed it.

"Let's try this," Porky says, taking the module from Dana's hands, which feel insanely large. Mickey Mouse hands. Not Minnie. Somehow not hers. Donald Duck feet. Goofy teeth. She runs her tongue over her molars and they do feel like silly little lumps of sharp in her mouth.

Louise follows Porky and breathes into the machine. Dana's is the only result indicating reduced pulmonary function. She tries again and while she feels no different, her ribs don't want to expand. They prefer not to. They're settled where they are and desire to float without interference.

The sun sets and Dana lounges bonelessly against Ben's warmth while Porky builds a fire in the hearth. Then he and Louise pile together in the corner of the sofa, orange light flickering over his pale skin and her frizzy hair. Her blue toenails glow electric.

Dana is tired as Ben pulls her to her feet. She reaches for her cane, but he slips an arm around her waist. "I gotcha, PharmD."

"Where are we going?"

"To bed."

"Oh my," Dana says with a coy hand over her mouth. "Taking me to bed, are you?"

"Unless you wanna sleep on the floor."

"I can go home."

"You're too fucked up to drive," he says as they make their way up and out of the living room.

"I'll call a Boober."

He pauses near the foyer. "If that's what you want."

She doesn't want. What she does want is to continue hanging off his wiry body exactly like this. But maybe she should go before she blurts something thoughtless and everyone is once again treating her like a vector of contagion. "What do *you* want, Ben?"

"Stay," he says, holding her closer. "Stay with me."

She nods, and it's the entire earth tilting. "Yes."

They stumble down the hall, Dana veering into Ben and smearing him along the wall. "Are you okay?" she asks. "Your lungs. You smoked a pot."

"Fine and dandy."

"I smoked pots."

"We need to work on your lingo." He pushes her through the door of his room. "You want a shirt or something?"

While Ben is rooting around in the dresser, she gets lost in her turtleneck before emerging victorious, dropping it to the floor like a pelt, then skinning out of her slacks to stand between the two ferns in her underwear. Ben emerges from his rummaging and blinks.

"Shit." His hand bunches into a fist around a grey t-shirt. "I take back what I said about your lab coat."

"That bad?" she teases, too stoned to care what a middle-aged woman's body looks like to a man in his twenties.

"You're killing me here, PharmD."

"Sorry, but I sleep in the nude."

"Could you make an exception tonight?"

"Why?" She reaches to unhook her bra.

Ben lunges forward, pushing the t-shirt into her chest. "Don't make this harder."

"Are you hard?"

"I'm gonna do my nebulizer," he says. "When I get back, please be in that shirt."

Dana hums happily as he trundles out with his tank and mask. Teasing aside, her limbs are heavy, her head floaty, and that waterbed is looking squishy delightful. She finds her way into the shirt and under the covers. A yellow shaft of light from the hall spears the darkness when Ben returns. Dana closes her eyes, listening to him put the tank away, and the rustle of cloth as he undresses, and the muted gurgle of the bed as he slides in beside her. Without thinking about it she snuggles into his arms.

Snuggling. Like a rabbit. Not something she knew she could do.

Or even knew how to do.

"Dana?"

"Ben."

"Thanks for coming over."

"I like it here."

She yawns as he strokes the length of her spine with his thumb. "Ben?"

"Dana."

"This is the best night of my life."

He whispers into her hair, "You wanna kiss for a while?"

"Yes."

They fold in and out of each other's arms like human origami and his toothpaste mouth finds hers. Their bodies don't grind. Their tongues don't connect. The opposite of the greenhouse effect, which left her on edge and confused. Soft. Safe. And she drifts away on a warm ocean, completely free of pressure points.

The next morning Dana slips out of bed, trying not to set off a tsunami that'll wake Ben. She dresses in the dark, and washes her face in the bathroom, feeling rested and quiet inside. Neither Porky nor Louise are up yet and she moves quietly so as not to disturb them. Dana is an expert at stealth exits, but this time she's not sneaking out. In the foyer, she finds a glass bottle in her left shoe. Unscrewing the dropper cap, the aromas of rosemary, peppermint, and lavender waft out.

She clutches the bottle to her chest. "Thank you, Francis."

It's Monday morning and the shop is closed, but nevertheless someone is waiting when she arrives, bringing to an abrupt end the most blissful morning-after she's ever experienced.

"Constable Partridge?"

Partridge grins. "Just Ted. Off duty."

"Me too." Dana pulls out her keys, hoping they don't tremble in her hand.

Ted nods to the CLOSED ON MONDAYS sign. "Both married to the job, I guess?"

Dana disarms the system with her app and unlocks the door.

"What brings you here today, Ted?"

"In the area. Thought I'd stop in and ask how your friend is doing."

"After you spoke with Callum."

Ted's smile doesn't waver. "Word travels, I guess."

"Why not ask Ben himself?"

"Like I said, just in the area." Ted thumbs the belt loops on her Costco dad jeans. "And my back."

"Your back?"

"You mentioned alternatives the first time I came in, when you thought I was a junkie."

"I never—"

"Ben seems like a fella in pain, Dana. He must take a lot of meds. For his health issues."

"Constable." Dana slices open a smile of her own. "I can't give you that information. Ethically or legally."

"And I wouldn't ask, not without the proper paperwork."

"Is there anything I can do for you today? Alternatively?"

"Don't guess there is," Ted says. "Glad to hear Mr. Kidd is feeling better. You take care of yourself, Dana. Whatever he's got, you don't wanna be catching it."

An idea jolts Dana awake just before 3 a.m. She lays on her back, staring up into the dark.

This could work. Maybe... No, it absolutely... This is something. Could be something. An alternative. For her. For all of them. Dana rolls over and grabs her phone; its blue glare slaps the oyster shell walls and stings her sleep-dilated irises. Opening her contacts, her finger hovers over the number. First time for everything. And 3 a.m. is as good a time as any.

The mall parking lot is a plowed asphalt wasteland, deserted but for Dana's Corolla and a Volvo station wagon in the far corner by the bus shelter. Ben penguin-walks carefully across the blacktop, skirting a patch of ice polished to a deadly shine.

"Thanks for coming," she says.

"Thanks for not being my mom. I almost didn't answer the phone."

"I could have picked you up."

He shrugs and shivers in his too thin coat. "Nice night for a walk."

"You had the right idea all along, Ben. A value-added product."

"Huh?"

"Cannabis is legal."

"I don't get it..." His quizzical grogginess lingers, then gives way to a flash of realization. "The secret ingredient is still behind the counter though. Are you breaking bad on me?"

"No," Dana says. "I'll still fill the Adderall, and assume you're taking it as prescribed. I'm talking about cannabis with supplemental organic preparations that enhance the consumer experience. Lavender for relaxation, peppermint for sinus congestion, ginger for nausea. We'd have to be careful about the language but..."

"Dana, to make a buck selling weed, especially legally, you gotta scale the operation to—"

"But you don't, that's the beauty of it, while the others go big box, we go boutique. Artisanal. Locally sourced, farm to table. You've already got the damn farm."

"Right," Ben says, but there's less reticence and more curiosity. "How do we get it to the stoners' table?"

Dana grips her cane and grins, gesturing to the darkened front of the mall. "Know any place where you tend to see a lot of stoners?"

Ben is silent for a long moment. Then he coughs a plume of fog into the air. "Shit, this could actually be something."

"I've been looking into the licensing, for the shop," Dana says. "I can dispense on behalf of a corporate grower. But our target customers are already here. Shoppers is closing in a couple months. I'll open up a second location. And maybe similar business will follow. We could bring this place back to life as an indoor farmer's market with a Wok-Wok. What do you think?"

Ben rubs his palms together, pondering the matter, then slides his cold hands into the collar of her jacket and moves in, his lips hovering inches from hers. "You ought to take me home, PharmD."

She nods.

He nods with her.

As they pull out of the parking lot, Dana notices the Volvo's lights flick on and a gust of fog erupt from the tail. She doesn't need to wonder who might have followed her to the mall in the middle of the night. She says nothing to Ben, but perhaps she'll be paying Constable T. Partridge a visit soon.

As they tiptoe noisily into the house, Dana is breathless, blood trilling through her arteries as the possibilities build upon each other, stacking up like beautiful storm clouds. Ben's cheeks are flushed peachy red and he's on her, all over her, hustling her into the living room, pushing her down on the couch with his body, his mouth. This is not slow, but it's not rushed. It's something else. Intent. Ben is kissing her with intention.

"You're sexy when you talk about running a scam," he breathes into her. "You need to abandon your ethics more often."

"It's not a scam," she laughs. "But I understand how going legit could seem that way to you."

Reaching under her tunic, he tugs at her leggings.

A cold dart sends a chill into her overheated blood. "Ben, what about—"

"They just started the *Rats of NIMH* game. They'll be at it for hours."

The leggings come off, and her underwear follows. Ben sinks to his knees on the floor, hands pressing into her thighs, pushing them apart.

"Wait," she says. "I don't know..."

"And we won't. Not until we try."

She clenches her fists. "I don't want to ruin us."

"Don't think about what happens out there," he says, holding her with his eyes and his arms, communicating tenderness as much as desire. "You're here. We're different. Everything we do together will be different."

She nods, and the warmth rushes back in. "Okay."

The first touch of his tongue is like a shock from a nine-volt battery. He goes slow, maddeningly slow, observing and adjusting, sweeping in and pulling back. Nudging her closer but not close enough.

"Ben," she gasps, "please."

"Whatever you say, PharmD."

She keeps her eyes open, fighting it, wanting it, dreading it, letting it sink in and blast out.

"Ben," she finally sighs and looks down between her legs. His head is still. She sits up and he crumples to the floor. Smears of red streak her thighs, and his face. Did she get her period? The momentary mortification is swept away when Ben coughs and more pinky-red foam dribbles from his greying lips. "Ben?"

It's as though she's gone deaf, leaving only faint suction around the edges of silence. She must be screaming. She stomps hard on the floor three times, then kneels on her broken patella. Tilting Ben's head back, she scoops the foam, like a bloody confection, out of his mouth. Then Porky is beside her, both of them naked from the waist down as they work on Ben, performing CPR by rote while Louise is on the phone, presumably with 911. Dana hears nothing, feels nothing, except for Louise's steady hand on her shoulder.

At some point the paramedics arrive.

At some point they leave.

Ben is gone.

On the couch, Porky holds Louise.

But Ben is gone.

Someone has wrapped a blanket around Dana, wiped the bloody foam off her hands and face—though she still feels it between her thighs. Ben's blood. Like she gave birth to him.

And now he's gone.

Ted Partridge wanders into the pharmacy on a windy March evening. It's been almost three months since Ben died. Like everything and everyone from that brief time, Dana can barely lift the hatch on that cellar of memory.

"Ted," Dana says, toneless.

"Dana."

"Picking up or dropping off?"

"Today? Neither," Ted replies. "I probably should have stopped in a lot sooner, but I wanted to say I'm real sorry for your loss. How've you been keeping?"

Dana's gaze flicks to Marge, restocking shelves with vitamin supplements. Telepathically begging for her to interrupt this conversation.

"I guess, I was wrong about you," Ted says.

Dana continues entering her orders into the computer. "Depends what you think you were wrong about."

"I thought you two...well, as I mentioned, Mr. Kidd wasn't exactly unknown to police."

"And you suspected me of diverting controlled substances for trafficking purposes."

"Guess I did."

"For the frequency with which you use the word," Dana says. "I'd *guess* you don't do much guessing at all, Ted." She looks up, expecting a steely glare. Instead, there are tears on Ted's ruddy cheeks. Dana can only stand frozen in shock as this formidable fortress of a human openly weeps in her pharmacy.

With a blunt hand, Ted wipes the tears away. "Apologies."

Dana rounds the counter and steps down from the dispensary platform. Eye to eye, she says, "Tell me. Tell me everything."

Marge graciously offers to close on her own. Dana and Ted depart in separate cars, and reunite at the mall. Over a clamshell of noodles for Dana and wonton soup for Ted, the whole story comes out.

"It's my wife," she says. "Kelsey. She's got rheumatoid arthritis. Like a burning knot of wood in every joint. Docs come under fire for opioids lately. Well, they cut her off. No more Oxy. Told her to fucking meditate instead. Take fish oil pills. Buy a TENS machine. Like we hadn't already tried it all. She always said it would be better if it were cancer, and now I get it." Ted swallows her last wonton. "Worst thing about that kind of pain? It won't actually fucking kill you."

"I'm so sorry." Dana surprises herself by reaching out and squeezing one of Ted's hands.

"The pills are poison, but at least they let her be a person for a few hours. And now she's talking about...you know, ending things. That's when I decided to develop a back problem." Ted chews purposefully and puts her spoon down. "I was never looking to bust you. Just make you think I was, so maybe..."

Dana shakes her head. "Ted, I've only ever filled legit scripts."

"I guess." Ted halts. "I mean, I know."

"I wish I could help." Even as she speaks the words, a quiet part of her memory begins to shout. A greenhouse and a hundred blooming ladies all named the same... She owes this to Ted, for her compassion toward Ben, for Ben's compassion toward anyone living in a world that didn't understand them. "I can't promise anything, but I might have a contact...an alternative."

Ted's eyes redden and well up again, and Dana feels the sting in her own tear ducts. Ted squeezes her hand. The touch, that simple, undemanding human contact Dana knew for only a short time, yet it changed her undeniably. She knows what she has to do.

There's no turning back the clock. Now is now. Standing on the front porch though, finger poised to ring the bell, Dana is angry all over again. Angry still, if she's being honest. Even after three months alone, haunting her soulless condo, trying to process, to

82

grieve, to forget and forgive. That lying little fuck. And he wasn't the only one. Porky knew. Louise knew. But no one told her until it didn't matter anymore.

Cystic fibrosis.

Congestive heart failure.

How had she not twigged on it? The nebulizer, the pancreatic enzyme replacement. The goddamn vest. It wasn't a life jacket as she'd stupidly thought, but a medical device, for high-frequency oscillation therapy, to keep his lungs clear. Lungs that filled with backed up blood from a heart that had worked too hard, for too long.

He had the gall to moan about every conceivable illness of the imagination and hide the one terminal condition he actually had. He had the temerity to want something more than a life waiting to die.

He wanted to bloom.

She rings the bell, knowing Louise will likely spit on her for ghosting them after the funeral. But it's Porky who answers. He invites her inside and they sit in the living room. Same stone fireplace, orange couch, wild jungle planters. Porky doesn't take off his robe.

"Where's Louise?"

"Sleeping," he says. "She sleeps most of the time."

Now Dana sees the plants in the arboretum are drooping, wilting, dying without Ben's daily attention. Tears melt her vision and she lets them fall unreservedly. In this house, she wouldn't know how to be reserved.

"I'm so...so sorry, Francis."

He sighs. "Call me Porky. Everyone does."

"You know?"

"Of course I know. You're the only one who didn't. Someone should have told you."

Dana sniffs and nods.

"Took you long enough." Louise steps down into the living room, her hair matted, months of bereavement sharpening her exquisite curves. She falls down on the couch next to Porky. "How've you been, slut?"

"I...terrible, to be honest."

Dana observes Louise and Porky's platonic intimacy, and misses it like she'd miss a foot, or her ears, or a heart.

This ecosystem Ben cultivated, she's a part of it, and the plants need care, they're why she came back. It's the most important thing.

She turns to Louise and Porky.

"When can I move in?"

ACKNOWLEDGEMENTS

This story started as a vivid dream, and would not have made it onto these pages without the guidance and support of too many people to name, but here goes: my editor, Charlotte Hayes-Clemens, for her meticulous and generous work; PJ Vernon, for saving this story from the trunk; Robert Bose for pandemic writing sprints and quarantine cocktails; and my family, for saving my life. Finally, a massive glitter-bomb of love for all the artists and odd ducks in my life. You are my people, and you are the most important thing.

ABOUT THE AUTHOR

Sarah L. Pratt is a curly hair gladiator, indie bookseller, and queer fictioneer living on Treaty 7 land in the Canadian prairies. She is the author of *Suicide Stitch: Eleven Tales* (EMP Publishing) a novel, *Infractus* (Coffin Hop Press) and co-author of *Wall of Fire* (The Seventh Terrace). When not reading, writing, or annoying the cat, she can be found outside, playing in the dirt.